School of Reckoning

Mila Lightfoot

ISBN: 1490963057

ISBN-13: 978-1490963051

DEDICATION

For Tatym

CONTENTS

Mila Lightfoot

PROLOGUE

HILLTOP HALL, 27 MAY 1867

"James, I need to speak with you. In private."

James Fenn, first Earl of Kingsley, followed his wife down the narrow corridor and into her private sitting room. He thought she looked incensed, and wondered what could have caused her annoyance. She was rather prone to eruptions of temper, and James always tried to beat a hasty retreat when he saw she was in one of her moods. But it looked like he was not going to be so lucky today.

"What is it I might help you with, my dear?" he asked timidly, as Lady Caroline slammed the door closed behind them.

Looking at him with an expression of utter disgust, she said, "You might start by keeping your perverted hands off the young servant girls."

James almost laughed at the wild accusation. He wondered for a moment if his wife might be having a joke. But her expression remained stony and he grasped frantically for something to say that would reassure her she was mistaken.

"My dear, darling Caroline! You know it is you I love and only you! What could possibly have given you such an outrageous idea?"

"Oh James," she said disdainfully, "I may be a woman, but I am not stupid. I saw you and that filthy scullery maid walking out of the woods together."

"Oh that!" exclaimed James, feeling relieved that he had a good explanation for being seen alone with the young girl. "Why I was only showing young Miriam that little cottage just beyond the woods. She told me she is looking for lodgings for her elderly mother and I suggested she have a look at the cottage which is simply standing empty at present."

Lady Caroline laughed scornfully.

"You really expect me to believe that, don't you James?" she said contemptuously. "Well I'll have you know that I won't stand for your philandering. You and that filthy little scullery rat had better be careful. Hell hath no fury like a woman scorned!"

HILLTOP HALL, SEPTEMBER 2012

CHAPTER 1
MY FAIR LADY

I'd been at Hilltop Hall School exactly a month. And I hated it. I'd never boarded before and I was used to a school that had both girls and boys - not just girls. They seemed so stuck-up and I was really struggling to make friends. I shared a room with a girl called Layla Smith-Bailey. She was pretty with long brown hair and big brown eyes. Her father was a prominent politician and she seemed to think herself superior to everyone else. She went on and on about all the trophies she'd won for show jumping and skiing, and she never stopped moaning about how she thought our room needed redecorating as it wasn't to her taste. She said things like, "I must speak to Father about this accommodation; it's really not up to standard. I don't know how one can be expected to live in these conditions."

You see Hilltop Hall is an independent school and the fees are outrageously high. My family could never have afforded to send me there, but I'd won a scholarship for doing well at my previous school, so that's how I'd ended up there, shortly after my fifteenth birthday.

Mum had said, "Lizzy, look at it this way. It's a huge opportunity. You'll get an excellent education that most girls could never have, and you'll be able to go on to one of the best universities."

My parents were so proud of me and so excited about the fact that I'd been accepted into Hilltop Hall that I felt I couldn't disappoint them. But it was really difficult; I felt so lonely.

The school is an imposing historic house which was built in the Jacobean era. Surrounded by ancient oak woods, it stands at the top of a hill, majestically surveying the countryside for miles around. The buildings are made of red brick, with gables, turrets and mullioned windows. When you stand in front of the school, it feels like you've stepped back in time. The views from the upper floors are amazing, but the interior is terribly cold and draughty. We had to wear vests and jumpers most of the year or we'd freeze! The rooms are huge, but the corridors are dark and sinister, with the odd wall sconce placed here and there to cast a bit of light. The whole place always felt spooky to me, especially if I happened to be walking down those corridors alone at night!

The Hilltop Hall school uniform was very smart, and the teachers made sure we always looked like 'young ladies,' as they put it. We wore purple and blue checked skirts (not too short), grey tights, black shoes, white blouses, grey school jumpers and grey blazers with the school badge on the front pocket. We also wore ties and scarves with our house emblems on them. It wasn't too bad, except for the straw boater hats! I found it near impossible to keep mine on my head because my unruly brown hair always caused it to lift up like a hot air balloon about to take off! Also, no jewellery was allowed except for a gold or silver stud in each ear and definitely, under no circumstances, was make-up to be worn. If our blouses were not tucked in, we got an instant detention, and if we went anywhere out of school, we had to wear those dreaded hats! Even worse were the rules about no mobile phones during the week and no surfing the internet. It definitely felt like I'd taken a step back in time!

There were three 'houses' at Hilltop Hall. They were called Churchill, Thatcher and Attlee, after famous British Prime Ministers. Churchill's colour was yellow, Thatcher was Red and Attlee was Blue. Churchill's emblem was an open book with a cross behind it, Thatcher's was a horse's head, and Atlee's was an oak tree. These three emblems appeared together on the school badge. I was in Attlee, so I stayed in Attlee house. Our house mistress was Mrs Tupperley, a massive, stern woman with short grey hair and a triple chin. Nothing got past Mrs Tupperley; I think she had eyes at the back of her head!

We had all the usual lessons at Hilltop Hall, as well as some unusual ones. We could choose between certain non-essential subjects such as Music, Herbology, Photography, Pottery and Dressmaking. I chose Herbology, as I thought it sounded the most interesting. We also had sports such as hockey, horse riding, indoor swimming, croquet, athletics and lacrosse.

I soon got used to all the rules and regulations, and I hadn't had a detention yet. I was also doing quite well in my lessons, but what I really wanted were some friends!

My favourite lessons were English and Art. I've always loved anything creative, where I can let my imagination run free. Our Art teacher was Miss Mason, and she always made our lessons really interesting. On that particular Friday, she told us about a new project that we'd be doing in groups. I was secretly pleased when Miss Mason put us into groups herself because I knew no one would have chosen me otherwise.

"Right," she said, "I'd like Beatrice, Lizzy, Layla, Meredith and Cassie to work together."

The other girls looked at each other and smiled, happy to have been put in the same group. They glanced at me briefly, then started whispering amongst themselves. I knew Layla because we shared a room, and I'd met Cassie because she and Layla were best friends. Cassie, a beautiful girl with long wavy blonde hair and huge blue eyes, was also in Attlee. I secretly thought it was fortunate for her good looks, because as far as intelligence went - well let's just say she wasn't exactly the brightest bulb on the Christmas tree. I'd never spoken to Beatrice or Meredith. Beatrice was a plump girl, with mousy blonde hair which she always wore tired up in a ponytail. Meredith was a very tall girl who had shoulder length brown hair cut in a bob, hazel eyes, and a face that seemed to be set in a permanent scowl. I found her very intimidating.

After dividing the class into groups, Miss Mason briefed us on our assignment.

"I think you're going to enjoy this project," she said. "Each group will make a papier mache model of the school, and I thought we'd display the best ones in the grand entrance foyer during the school's one hundredth birthday celebrations in December."

Everyone looked interested, and we were soon sitting around in our groups discussing how we would go about designing our models. Then Miss Mason suggested we go outside and sketch the school building from the grounds, so we made our way out into the lukewarm autumn sunshine.

Meredith happened to be standing near me while we worked, and I noticed her glancing sideways at me from time to time. I just was beginning to feel self-conscious when she looked directly at me and said, "Tell me - what is 'Lizzy' short for?"

"It's short for Eliza," I said with a smile, feeling pleased that someone was taking an interest in me at last.

Then she seemed to smirk and, with arched eyebrows, said, "Eliza. Hmm. That reminds me of a musical I once saw." And, looking smugly at the others, she asked in a sickly sweet tone, "Have any of you girls seen it? It's called My Fair Lady."

There were some snickers from the other girls and my face burned crimson from humiliation. I knew exactly what Meredith was getting at. My Fair Lady is a play based on a book called Pygmalion, by George Bernard Shaw. The story is about Eliza Doolittle, a bedraggled Cockney flower girl who takes speech lessons from Professor Henry Higgins, a phoneticist, so that she might pass as a well-born lady. I knew my accent wasn't posh like the other girls at Hilltop Hall, but this was the first time I realised that it actually made a difference as to how they perceived me.

Then Layla said spitefully, "Well who would have thought? Eliza Doolittle at Hilltop Hall!"

That led to an outburst of unrestrained laughter from most of the other girls, which sent me running miserably back in to school, burning with humiliation and more embarrassed than I'd ever felt in my entire life.

I stayed in my room until supper time, wondering despondently how I could face anyone after what had happened. But after I'd calmed down, and my anger and embarrassment had subsided somewhat, I decided to put things in perspective. Those girls were just having a bit of tactless fun, I reasoned. They've probably forgotten all about it by now, so I need to stop imagining the whole thing as such a big deal.

Feeling better, I cleaned myself up and went down to the dining room. But just as I sat down at one of the long tables, a girl I didn't know exclaimed loudly, "Oh, I say! Eliza Doolittle has decided to join us after all!"

My cheeks burned and my heart sank.

There was some snickering until Mrs Tupperley said, "Alright, settle down girls! You know I won't tolerate any unruly behaviour!"

That put a stop to it, but I hardly ate. I couldn't bring myself to look at anyone, so I sat with my head down, picking at my food and feeling like some novel curiosity.

I lay awake that night, wondering whether I should ring my mum and dad and tell them I'd had enough of Hilltop Hall School and was ready to pack my bags and come home. I certainly felt that way. But after tossing and turning for hours, mulling this dilemma over in my mind like a ship being tossed about by a stormy sea, I resolved to wait a bit longer and not say anything just yet.

I spent most of Saturday reading and learning for some upcoming tests. Then on Sunday the sun came out and I was feeling too confined in my room, so I decided to go for a walk in the grounds. The gardens were huge and beautiful, boasting elegant topiaries amid well-tended hedges. I squinted as the sun sparkled on the surface of a pond as I passed, creating dazzling beams of light on the water. Eventually I came to the edge of the old oak woods. I'd never ventured there before, but didn't feel like going back yet, so I wandered through the trees, crunching the dry leaves under my feet while watching squirrels scurry up and down. The woods felt deliciously cool and peaceful and I soon felt worlds away from my troubles. I ended up walking further than I'd planned - right to the far edge of the woods, where a long winding path led down the hill. I stood for a moment and admired the view. We weren't really allowed to wander this far, but I still wasn't in the mood to go back yet.

So I strolled down the path, which wound round a corner and past a rocky outcrop. I continued on, presently arriving at a little tumbledown cottage. It was made of stone and almost completely covered in ivy. I was surprised at my discovery, and wondered if anyone lived there. I walked up to the door, where a weathered plaque read: Cliodhna Cottage. *What a strange name,* I thought, trying to pronounce it by silently mouthing the words. Then I looked around and realised that someone must live there because it was surrounded by a well-tended garden and there were wisps of smoke coming from the chimney. So with my curiosity aroused, I crept around to one of the windows and peered in.

There inside a small room stood a tall woman with very long dark hair. She had her back to me, so I couldn't see what she was doing, but I could make out a table with some candles on it, and a strange five sided star within a metal circle hanging on the wall directly opposite where I stood. The sound of a dozen wind chimes then startled me as a sudden breeze caused them to tinkle and clang. I shrunk below the windowsill and noticed for the first time the many crystals and fairy ornaments which decorated the garden. What a peculiar place, I thought. But by then it was time to head back for lunch, so I tiptoed slowly away and back down the path towards the woods.

CHAPTER 2

TOADSTOOLS AND PENTAGRAMS

During assembly on Monday morning, Mrs Garnett, our head teacher, announced that one of our teachers, Miss Angelica, had returned after an unexpectedly prolonged holiday, so our Herbology lessons could now begin for the year. I'd never done Herbology but I thought it sounded quite interesting as well as a bit mysterious. So when the bell rang for our lesson, I went in and found a seat near the front of the classroom. The Herbology room had a conservatory joined on, which seemed to make it feel warmer than the rest of the school, probably because it was south facing and often had the sun on it. The conservatory was full of different plants, all growing haphazardly in different sized pots on metal shelves. I must admit I didn't think it looked very interesting, and that at that moment I was feeling somewhat less inspired about Herbology. Then everyone sat up as the teacher walked in.

"Good morning class, my name is Miss Angelica and I'll be your Herbology teacher this year," she said, smiling.

The class stood as one and said, "Good morning Miss Angelica."

Our teacher was tall and slim and had long hair the colour of a raven. She wore a brown and green dress, embellished with numerous tiny beads, and a necklace bearing a brownish coloured crystal hung round her neck. A queer scent lingered in the air around her - not like perfume or body spray, but more of a sweet, fragrant, spicy smell. Miss Angelica seemed familiar for some reason, but I couldn't think where I might have seen her before.

"Can anyone tell me what Herbology is?" she asked, looking expectantly around the room.

Blank faces stared back at her. "Okay," she continued, smiling valiantly, "let me tell you about this fascinating subject. Basically, Herbology is the study and use of herbs. The word herb applies to a wide variety of plants, including grasses, trees, shrubs, weeds, roots, barks, and the flowers of any plant used for healing, nutrition, magic spells and rituals, witchcraft, Wicca, and various other purposes."

A few of the girls' eyes widened at the mention of 'magic spells' and 'witchcraft', and Miss Angelica smiled contentedly as she realised she had the class's attention at last.

"Right," she said finally, "let's get started."

The lesson consisted mainly of Miss Angelica giving us a guided tour of the conservatory. I was amazed that she knew the name of each and every plant, as well as its many uses. By the end of the lesson I was totally fascinated by the interesting facts we'd learned about the different herbs. I mean who would have known that more people in the world use herbs today rather than conventional medicine? Or that Viking warriors used to ingest those pretty but poisonous red and white toadstools before going into battle, in order to become totally fearless! I pondered these things as the bell rang, then gathered up my things. I stole another glance at Miss Angelica. I knew I had seen her somewhere before, but I just couldn't think where.

I had acquired the unfortunate nickname of Eliza D, but because my surname was Dixon, the teachers never suspected the other students were making fun of me. There was nothing I could really do about it, so I let it go and reluctantly accepted it. I actually tried to act like it didn't bother me in the least. And it was around this time that I unexpectedly made my first friend at Hilltop Hall. A thin, pale-skinned girl with long, wavy auburn hair and vivid green eyes, Florence Knowles also attended the school on a scholarship. She was from a well off family, but her dad's business had recently collapsed, and her parents couldn't afford to pay the school fees. Flo and I had been paired up in geography class and we got along instantly. We had quite a lot in common and enjoyed the same subjects. I told her about the strange little cottage I'd found while out walking, and she begged me to show it to her the following weekend.

The week seemed to drag by slowly, and I felt tense about our Art lesson on Wednesday. I hated having to be in a group with those horrid, spiteful girls. I felt like they looked down on me and found bullying me entertaining. Eventually the lesson arrived and, taking our seats at a table near the window, we began the task constructing the school building out of pieces of cardboard and newspaper. It was really an enjoyable project and I soon became so immersed in my work that I almost forgot about the other girls.

But a few moments later Cassie looked up and said sweetly, "Oh

Eliza D, I forgot to mention something when I saw you the other day. Mother has been sorting through my clothes at home and has a few bags of hand-me-downs. She asked me what she should do with them and I thought of you. They're all designer, so you'd be really lucky to get them."

The other girls smirked. My face turned crimson and I couldn't think of anything to say. My blood was boiling and I felt like slapping Cassie right across her pretty little spiteful face. My hand itched to do it, but I knew that such an act would certainly result in my permanent exclusion.

Then Meredith said, "Cassie, that's so considerate of you. I do admire people who give to charity." And, looking straight at me, she said, "Eliza D, I would be very grateful if I were you. You are lucky to be acquainted with such kind and thoughtful people like our dear Cassie."

Taking a deep breath and pulling myself together, I looked up, smiled brightly and said (very sarcastically), "Why you're right! I'm ever so lucky to have met such a wonderful group of astonishingly nice girls! You are all the personification of kindness!"

That seemed to shut them up for the time being, and I went back to work with a smile on my face, much to their annoyance.

By the time Friday came round I was more than ready for the weekend. Our last lesson of the week was Herbology and as I relaxed back at my desk, I thought, *only an hour to go before the bell.* Then in walked Miss Angelica and suddenly, like a bolt of lightning, it struck me where I'd seen her before! She was the woman I had seen in the little cottage on the edge of the wood. She was tall and thin and had that really long, dark hair! So Miss Angelica lived in that peculiar little tumbledown cottage! As I thought about it, it made perfect sense. Of course an eccentric woman like Miss Angelica would live in a place like that!

The lesson went by quickly, with Miss Angelica explaining the medicinal uses of the most common herbs. We did a worksheet and then the bell rang. I hurriedly went to find Flo so we could discuss our weekend plans. I found her waiting impatiently in the corridor outside my room.

"There you are Lizzie!" she exclaimed. "What took you so long?"

"Flo you know the Herbology room is way over the other side of the building! Now come on, let's discuss our plans!"

So we lounged around in my room, listening to music and chatting happily 'til supper time. I told Flo about Miss Angelica and how she was the person who lived in that funny little cottage with the strange name at the edge of the woods.

After breakfast on Saturday morning, we set off through the grounds. It was a lovely autumn day, with only a few small, puffy clouds like bits of cotton wool in the sky. We had entered the woods and were strolling among the ancient oaks when Flo suddenly stopped and crouched down in front of a toadstool.

"Look Lizzy!" she said. "Aren't these little red and white mushrooms pretty?"

"No don't touch that! I shouted. "Miss Angelica taught us about those. They're toadstools and they're called —wait, let me think - Fly

Agaric! They're poisonous and if you eat them really strange and horrible things can happen to you. You could hallucinate or even die!"

Flo looked shocked and stood up at once. Grimacing, she asked, "Did you learn that in Herbology?"

"Yes", I replied, "I suppose some of it really can come in useful in real life!"

And with that we continued on our way until we came to the little cottage with the well-tended, fairy-like garden.

"Oh it's sweet!" gushed Flo.

"I suppose it is in a way," I said thoughtfully.

Then we nearly jumped out of our skin as a black cat appeared from nowhere, brushing up against our legs and meowing loudly.

"Oh my heart!" exclaimed Flo, clutching her chest. "Where did it come from? It gave me such a fright!"

We giggled nervously and made our way to the front door of the cottage. It had obviously been painted many years ago, because the old green paint was peeling off in ragged lines, revealing the bare wood underneath. We had decided to pay Miss Angelica a little visit, as we were quite curious about her and the mysterious little house. I knocked on the door and it was soon opened by Miss Angelica, who looked very surprised to see us.

"Oh!" she said, somewhat startled. "And what brings you two young ladies to my humble abode?"

"Good morning Miss Angelica," I said politely. "It's such a lovely day that my friend Florence and I decided to go for a walk. We were following the path through the woods, and it led us to this little cottage, so we decided to see who lived here."

Miss Angelica smiled warmly and invited us in. As we entered, I looked around and remembered the metal circle on the wall with the five-sided star in it. At the far side of the room was a small table covered with a dark patterned cloth. On it were four candles, three of them white and one black. They were all lit, which seemed a bit strange in the daytime, especially when the sun was shining brightly. There were also two statues of peculiar looking people, a bowl of shiny stones, a burning stick of incense which gave off a strong, sweet smell, and a smaller one of those circles with the five-sided star in it. I also noticed an unusual stick and a large cup - a bit like a wine glass but bigger, and made of shiny silver metal.

What an odd assortment of things, I thought to myself.

Flo and I must have been staring wide-eyed at everything, because after an expectant silence, Miss Angelica said, "I see you two are admiring my little altar."

Flo and I nodded awkwardly.

"It's beautiful, isn't it?" she went on. "Really special. A place where I can feel at one with nature and the universe."

"Umm," I said, feeling the need to say something, "what's that star in the circle? I see you have one on the wall as well as that smaller one on your, um, altar."

"Oh yes, that's something interesting," she said enthusiastically. "It's called a Pentagram. The upward point of the star is representative of the spirit. The other four points all represent an element: earth, air, fire, and water. All these things contribute to life and are a part of each of us. Look," she went on, holding up her necklace, "I'm wearing a pentagram at the moment. When you wear one of these you feel connected with the elements as well as the earth and all creation."

"That really is very interesting Miss Angelica," said Flo, looking uneasy. "But Lizzy and I have to go now. We don't want to be late for lunch and it's quite a walk back."

Miss Angelica nodded and smiled, telling us to please pop around again soon for a cup of tea and some homemade biscuits. We thanked her and made our way out.

Once in the woods, Flo turned to me and, putting her hands on my shoulders, said, "Lizzie! Do you realise Miss Angelica's a witch?"

"A witch?" I asked incredulously, and couldn't help but laugh. "Oh come on Flo, you have got to be joking!"

But Flo looked dead serious. "You saw the altar, right? With the candles and the incense and that Pentagram thing and the wand…"

"What's wrong with incense?" I asked sceptically. "And lots of people burn candles. As for a wand, I did see a kind of stick but - come on Flo, there's no such thing as witches in real life!"

Flo looked around and spotted a mossy old tree stump.

"Come Lizzy," she said, looking frustrated. "Let's sit down here for a few minutes."

So we both took a seat on the cold, hard stump and Flo began to explain why she thought Miss Angelica was a witch.

"I've read lots of books about witches," she said. "It's a known fact that they do spells at those altars! That's why they have all those odd looking things like statues and crystals and incense and stuff. Did you notice that big cup? That's called a chalice. And the wand! I know a wand when I see one!"

I was thoughtful for a while, because Flo did sound very sincere.

"Okay," I said eventually, "you do seem to know a lot about these things. But I'm still not completely convinced. I think I need some more evidence."

CHAPTER 3

POSH PRANKS

The next few weeks brought colder weather, along with wind and rain, which seemed to make everyone a bit down in the mouth. The trees were now almost bare and the sky was grey and oppressive. The school's one hundredth birthday was coming up, and there was lots of extra work to do in order to get everything ready for the big day. The teachers wanted to display our best artwork on the walls, and in English class we were working on poems, the best of which would be chosen for us to read to the visitors. We were also practicing songs to sing at a big assembly on the day.

Flo and I hadn't had a chance to visit Miss Angelica again, but were planning to soon. In the meantime, we were working hard at school and I was thrilled with how my poem was coming along. I didn't say anything to anyone, but I was so hoping Mrs Stokes would choose me to read it to the visitors.

Then one evening, when I was stretched out on my bed, deep in concentration while trying to finish off some homework, I became aware of Layla's voice. I looked up at her and frowned.

"What does it take to get your attention?" she exclaimed. "I've been calling your name for the past five minutes!"

"Oh I'm sorry," I stammered. "I was just really absorbed in this work."

"Oh, okay," she shrugged. "Anyway, a few of us girls are going riding tomorrow afternoon, and we wondered if you'd like to join us."

To say I was surprised by this unusual invitation would be an understatement. I thought my ears must be deceiving me. Leila obviously sensed my astonishment and smiled sweetly.

"Come on Eliza!" she said pleasantly. "Some of us were saying how it's about time we included you in something."

"B,b,but," I stammered, "I've never even ridden a horse. I wouldn't know what to do!"

"Oh don't worry about that," said Layla reassuringly. "I'll make sure you get to ride the smallest, quietest horse. How does that sound?"

I really wanted to believe her. I wanted so badly to be accepted. Could it be possible that the popular girls were ready to accept me at last, and wanted to include me in their leisure activities? I really, really hoped so, and, putting all doubts to the back of my mind, I happily accepted the invitation.

I was quite surprised at the change in attitude that Layla and her friends exhibited the following day. They smiled and said 'hello' when they saw me, and I was secretly over the moon. But Flo was very suspicious. She called me aside as soon as she noticed.

"What's going on?" she demanded.

I tried to feign surprise. "What do you mean?" I asked casually.

"Oh I think you know exactly what I mean!" she argued. "Why are those normally horrid girls being so nice to you today?"

I looked away angrily. I couldn't believe Flo's attitude. Then I turned and looked her straight in the eyes.

"And why shouldn't they be nice to me?" I asked snappily. "Why is it so unbelievable to you that I might actually be liked by the popular girls? Really, I thought you were my friend, Flo!"

"Lizzy," she said quietly, "I *am* your friend and I'm only trying to look out for you. I don't trust those girls. I think they may have an ulterior motive."

"Well thanks for your concern," I said sarcastically. "And by the way, if you're looking for me later, I'll be off riding with my new friends."

I must admit it felt deeply satisfying to see Flo's mouth drop open as I turned and walked off, grinning smugly.

Later that afternoon I met Layla, Cassie, Meredith and Beatrice down at the stables. There was also another girl with them who I'd seen in some of my classes, named Amanda Cartwright. She had extremely curly brown hair (even curlier than mine) and was very tanned, probably from some recent holiday in a warm, sunny place. The girls all greeted me warmly and Beatrice handed me some beige riding jodhpurs and a pair of long black leather boots to wear. Once I'd changed, Layla gave me a black velvet riding helmet and told me to try it on and see if the size was right.

When we were all ready, Meredith said authoritatively, "Alright girls, let's saddle up." Then she turned to me and said, "I'll be riding my horse, Storm, Layla will be on Blaze, Cassie on Topaz, Amanda on Gypsy Star and Beatrice on Prince. You'll be riding Bramble. She's such a darling; you'll love her."

After collecting our saddles and bridles from the tack room, we went to our horses' stables and set about getting them ready. Beatrice showed me how to brush Bramble and use a hoof pick to get the dirt out of her hooves. Then Meredith came over and told me she would be happy to help by putting Bramble's saddle on for me. I was thankful for that, because I had no idea how to put on a saddle.

Soon everyone was ready and we led our horses out of their stables and into a small courtyard. I marvelled at how big Storm was - he looked huge and was prancing around like a racehorse. Layla's horse, Blaze, was really beautiful. He was dark brown with white 'stockings' on all his legs and a white blaze down his face. The other horses also looked very smart, especially compared to dumpy little Bramble, who was brown and white, like a cow. She also seemed like a bit of a grumpy old thing, trying to bite my arm as I led her out the stable.

As it was already dark outside, we took the horses over to the spacious indoor arena. It was well-lit and had a sand floor and mirrors lining one whole wall. I wondered why people needed to admire themselves while they were riding. Then I noticed the girls were getting onto their horses, so I thought I should do the same. I was just about to put my foot into the stirrup to hoist myself up onto Bramble's back, when I heard a noise behind me.

"Lizzy, wait!" shouted Flo, looking frantic. "Don't get on!"

I stood and stared as she ran breathlessly up to me. "Look," she said gravely, "your girth's loose! The minute you put your weight in that stirrup, the saddle will slip right around, and you'll end up head first on the ground under your horse's belly!"

***

That evening I sat cross-legged on Flo's bed, feeling despondent. It was really cold and I had a fleece blanket wrapped snugly around my shoulders.

"How did you know about the loose girth?" I asked at last.

"Well firstly," said Flo, "I told you I didn't trust those girls. And secondly, I had my own pony a couple of years ago, so I know what to look out for."

"I don't even want to think about what would've happened if you hadn't turned up when you did," I said miserably. "I can't believe those girls! And I can't believe I actually fell for their horrid little prank. I'm so stupid! And I'm so, so sorry I said all that mean stuff to you. "

"You should just try to forget all about it," Flo said kindly. "Just ignore those girls completely. Don't give them the time of day. They're not worth it."

I agreed with my friend, but to be honest I was burning with anger inside. And the more I thought about the whole thing, the angrier I became. That night I lay awake thinking about revenge. I wanted to get back at them. My mind was full of malicious thoughts as I lay tossing and turning, unable to sleep. Maybe if Flo hadn't turned up when she did, I thought, I would have ended up being kicked by that grumpy old horse, and those girls would have been permanently excluded from school. But I knew deep down they'd probably have got away with it, by saying it was an accident. Well into the early hours, I continued to think about how to get revenge, but I just couldn't seem to come up with a realistic plan that could actually be carried out - and that wouldn't result in death or permanent injury!

The next morning I felt shattered. I was so tired, my eyes were red and puffy and I could feel a headache coming on. That was my reward for a night of hateful fantasies, and I certainly wasn't in the best of moods. The first lesson (maths) passed in a dreary blur, and I was relieved when the bell rang. Then in English, I realised to my dismay that I'd left my poem up in my bedroom. Mrs Stokes, who was known for being strict, wasn't very pleased with me but at least I wasn't punished. I think she let me off for this one little incident because I was one of the best students in her class.

The last lesson of the day was Herbology, and I walked into the classroom stifling a yawn. It wasn't that I found the subject boring - it was just by that stage I was so exhausted that keeping my eyes open was becoming a challenge. Then when Miss Angelica walked in, she looked so bright and full of enthusiasm that I actually felt my lethargy start to dissolve.

She smiled brightly as she said, "Right girls! I'd like to do something interesting with you today, so we'll be looking at a different side of Herbology. So far we've done some botany and learned about the various ways herbs can maintain and improve our health. Today we're going to have a look at the magical properties of herbs."

The magical properties of herbs? I thought, as whatever was left of my tiredness evaporated, and I sat up and listened intently. Miss Angelica went on to tell us that in magic, parts of herbs such as roots, stems, leaves and flowers are used for several different purposes. We learned that herbs can be used for purification, protection, banishing, divination, evoking and spell casting. Miss Angelica was just getting into her stride when she was interrupted by a girl named Willow, who had raised her hand.

"With all due respect Miss," said Willow, with a look of disbelief, "is this like, for real? I mean…magic?" She said the word 'magic' with a look of extreme scepticism. "Everyone knows there's no such thing as magic in real life. This kind of stuff belongs at Hogwarts, not Hilltop High."

There was a lot of giggling in response to this, but Miss Angelica didn't look at all bothered.

"My dear child," she said kindly, "magic is very real and has existed as a precise science for thousands of years. Every single person can learn to do magic. The only reason it seems so bizarre and unusual is that this society no longer teaches the art and science of magic. In the distant past, magical study was just as important as maths, science or the arts. And herbs are used abundantly in magic, even today."

Then she looked at the rest of us and smiled broadly. "Believe it girls," she said assuredly. "A spell can achieve almost anything you can imagine."

I was fascinated and hung on every word Miss Angelica said until the end of the lesson. Then as soon as the bell rang I dashed off to find Flo.

"You're not going to believe this!" I whispered excitedly, before relating the details of my extraordinary Herbology lesson. Flo listened wide-eyed and then nodded.

"I knew it!" she said after a pause. "I knew Miss Angelica was a witch. How else would she know all that stuff about casting spells with herbs?"

"I think you might just be right," I said.

Flo and I talked until supper time. We decided it was time to pay Miss Angelica another visit. The next day was Saturday and we had no plans, so that would be perfect. That night, as I lay in bed trying to fall asleep, Miss Angelica's words echoed in my head: A spell can achieve almost anything you can imagine.

***

Saturday dawned cold and grey, but at least it was dry. I met Flo in the courtyard after breakfast.

"Look!" she said, twirling around. "Miss Kelly said we could start wearing our scarves now it's got so cold."

"Very nice," I said, admiring her purple and blue striped scarf embroidered with the 'Churchill' motif. "I wonder when old Mrs Tupperley will let us start wearing ours. It's freezing!"

And with that we started towards the woods. As we walked, a thick, menacing fog crept in, making the day seem even darker. The atmosphere began to take on an eerie quality and I shivered, partly from the cold and partly from our spooky surroundings. I turned and looked back at the school, which now resembled the outline of a huge, menacing monster, only just visible in the distance. As we entered the woods, the only sound was the crunching of dry leaves underfoot, the sound of which was amplified in the dead quiet, still air. It felt like we were in another world, where the trees and fog were shutting us in, reluctant to let us go. Then as we got deeper into the woods, a squirrel suddenly scampered up a tree beside me and I screamed in fright. Flo laughed.

"Feeling a bit spooked today are we?" she asked teasingly. "It must be the weather; it's so murky with the fog, and the woods do look a bit creepy now with the trees all bare."

I was thoughtful for a minute. "No, it's not that," I said shortly. "Well I'm sure that might have something to do with it, but I've had a weird feeling ever since my Herbology lesson yesterday. I went to bed last night thinking about magic and spells and witches and things."

Flo looked at me quizzically. "And?" she asked.

I bit my lip, hesitating. "Well," I said, "if magic is real - if it actually exists in real life…" I stared off into the distance, letting my voice trail off.

"Just what are you trying to say?" asked Flo, tilting her head to one side and furrowing her brow.

"I want to learn to do magic," I stated firmly. "Not the tricks you see on television. I'm talking about real magic. Spells and stuff."

As Flo listened, her expression became serious.

"I don't know Lizzy," she said at last. "I think real magic - if it does actually exist - can be dangerous. Like I said, I've read a lot of stories..."

Her sentence trailed off and she narrowed her eyes suspiciously until they became green, cat-like slits.

"Wait a minute," she said. "Why do you want to learn magic? What exactly are you planning to do with it?"

I looked at the ground and rustled some crinkly yellow leaves with my foot. Flo kicked me lightly on the shin to get my attention.

"Well?" she demanded, her green eyes now wide.

"Okay, okay!" I exclaimed. "But I think you might try to talk me out of it."

"Try me," said Flo, her eyes now cat-like slits again.

"Stop giving me your cat-eyes!" I grumbled. "I want to learn to do spells so I can get back at those awful stuck-up bullies."

Flo looked contemplative.

"I think I see where you're coming from," she said at last. "Don't get mad - get even."

CHAPTER 4

HARM NONE, DO AS YOU WILL

The little cottage looked rather dismal in the swirling fog. Smoke rose from the chimney and the garden looked vacant and forlorn. As we approached the old green door, we heard a meow and looked down to see Miss Angelica's black cat trotting enthusiastically towards us. I knelt down and stroked her, gently caressing her gorgeously soft and silky coat. Then I looked up as the door opened unexpectedly - we hadn't even knocked!

"Girls!" exclaimed Miss Angelica, who was wrapped up in a thick, colourful knitted shawl. "Welcome to Cliodhna Cottage! How lovely to see you again! Do come in out of the cold."

The little cottage was cosy and welcoming, with a fire blazing in the hearth. The cat had shot through the door as soon as it opened and was now sitting on a cushion in front of the fire, washing herself and looking content. Miss Angelica gestured for us to sit down on a pair of well-worn chairs, which were covered with brightly coloured throws.

"Now how about some nice tea to warm up?" she asked kindly. "I have Rose, Chamomile, Ginger, Lemon, Nettle and my personal favourite: mixed berries."

I looked uncertainly at Flo, who said politely, "I'd love to try some Rose tea please."

I decided to go with the mixed berries, which seemed to please Miss Angelica, who went off busily into the kitchen. Glancing around the room, I noticed a beautiful, ornate bookcase containing a large assortment of books. Not being able to suppress my curiosity, I got up and went to take a look. One particular book immediately caught my eye, and I tilted my head to read the words on the well-worn spine. It was called The Complete Book of Spells. I gestured for Flo to come and have a look. She read the name and looked at me with wide eyes, apparently impressed with my discovery.

"I see you've found my treasured collection of books."

Miss Angelica's voice broke through our unspoken thoughts.

"Do you mind?" I asked innocently. "You seem to have some really interesting books here."

"Not at all," said Miss Angelica graciously. "You're welcome to look through them but do take care as some are very old, and there are more than a few rare collectors' items amongst them."

We thanked her and sat down to have our tea. It was my first time drinking herbal tea and I thought it tasted sweet and refreshing. Miss Angelica also set out a plate of homemade biscuits. She said they were Lavender flavour, and I noticed they had little purple bits in them, which I assumed were from the Lavender flowers. They tasted delicious. While we ate, I asked Miss Angelica what the name of her cottage meant.

"Oh!" she exclaimed, "I'm so glad you asked! It's a name of Irish origin mentioned in folklore. You don't pronounce the 'd', so it's actually 'Clee-uh-na' or 'Clee-oh-na', depending on your accent. Anyway, Cliodhna was a fairy woman who had magical birds whose songs could heal the sick. Isn't that lovely? Although the story also goes that she fell in love with a mortal and followed him to his world. Then Manannan, god of the sea, created a huge wave that carried her back into the fairy world. But I think it's all rather romantic."

Miss Angelica sipped her tea and gazed wistfully out the window, with a faraway look in her eyes. I thought she was probably lonely living all by herself in that secluded little cottage.

When we'd finished our tea and biscuits, Flo said, "Miss Angelica, I notice you have some books on magic. Would you mind if Lizzy and I had a look at some of them?"

Miss Angelica looked surprised. "Are you girls interested in magic?" she asked.

"Well," I said hesitantly, "I told Florence about that Herbology lesson we had yesterday, where you taught us about how herbs are used in real magic, and to be honest we're both quite intrigued and would like to learn more."

"I see," Miss Angelica said hesitantly. "Well I don't suppose it could do any harm. How about if I lend you one of my books, and after you've both read it, you can decide whether or not you're still interested in magic?"

We nodded enthusiastically and she went over and took a dark coloured, hard covered book from the bookcase. I noticed it had a red Pentagram on the cover. Then she handed me the book and we thanked her for the lovely tea and biscuits, put on our coats, and turned to leave.

"Girls," said Miss Angelica abruptly as we stepped out the door. "Be careful. If you have any questions, you know where to find me."

**

The library smelled of polished wood and musty old books. A fire was burning in the grand old fireplace, and as we made ourselves comfortable on a sofa in a secluded corner, I was surprised to find that the large, high-ceilinged room could feel quite snug. But being eager to explore the tantalising mysteries we imagined were hidden in A Beginner's Guide to Witchcraft, we quickly opened the book and began to read. This is what it said:

"Chapter One

Being a Witch

Witches have existed in every society of the world since ancient times. They have been associated with performing magic. But a witch's role went beyond the domain of magic only. She used to be the village apothecary or a doctor, who cured patients with her potions, herbs, stones, oils, massages, chants, and, of course, rituals and magic. Her magic comprised the use of wands, going into trance, reading omens and communicating with ghosts and spirits. She also interpreted voices, dreams and visions that her patients saw during night or even day.

The word 'witch' is used for both male and female practitioners of magic. Witchcraft is the study and use of magic and this magic comes from the Earth. Magic does not help anyone who has no respect for it, so it is important that you respect the 'powers that be' at all times. This is not a game, and spells should not be cast about like they are in some popular television shows. Power comes from years of experience. The more you practice, the better you will get.

Being a Witch takes a lot of effort, study and responsibility. Attuning with nature is vital to being a Witch. Witches worship Mother Earth or the God and Goddess, and follow a code of ethics: 'Harm None, Do As You Will.' Witches take full responsibility for their actions. They know that any misdeeds that they do will come back to them in some form, be it karma or the three fold law. Witches must always carefully consider the consequences of their actions, and what impact they may have on others."

We stopped reading and looked at each other.

"Let's just get to the part about how to do spells," I said impatiently.

"I don't know, Lizzy," said Flo uneasily. "It sounds like real magic could be quite complicated. And what about how your misdeeds can come back to you? Did you read that part? Doesn't that worry you?"

"Look Flo," I said, "it's not like I'm planning to do anything evil. All I want is a little revenge. I really don't think there's any great harm in that, do you?"

Flo shrugged and we turned to the chapter on spells. There were love spells, health spells, weather spells, beauty spells, luck spells, fertility spells, wealth spells, friendship spells and protection spells. But there was absolutely nothing to do with revenge or getting your own back.

I groaned and closed the book.

Flo opened it again, flipped through some pages and then put the book in my lap. I looked down at the open page. It said:

"Chapter 3
Types of Magic

Magic is not divided into types with regard to good or evil, or black and white. What makes it good or evil is not the kind of magic that you use, but the use to which you put it. It is a force that can be used for doing good or evil. The way that we use this force will determine whether it is black or white, not the actual magic itself. Therefore, magic as it stands is not divided. Its use, motives, applications, intent and objectives make magic black or white.

When people talk about white magic, they generally refer to spells which help or heal. It is not any more or less difficult than black magic, and even white magic spells can have consequences.

Practitioners of magic consider spells which fight against, or try to manipulate free will to be black magic. Because these spells try to adversely influence the life of others, they can be rather dangerous. Free will is considered by some as the strongest force in nature, so care should definitely be taken when dealing in this darker side of magic. It must also be remembered that the line between white and black magic can sometimes be fuzzy."

I finished reading and closed the book, deep in thought. Then I looked at Flo.

"What do you think?" I asked expectantly.

"I think you need to be very, very careful," she said earnestly.

CHAPTER 5

DON'T BOTHER COMING BACK

Monday morning brought the first snow flurries of winter and the school was abuzz with activity. Everything had to be ready by Friday for the school's one hundredth birthday celebrations. There was an air of expectancy as we took our seats in English class that day. Mrs Stokes was going to tell us who had been chosen to read their poems in front of all the students and visitors on Friday.

"Good morning girls," she said as she entered the room. "Isn't it cold today?"

We were then given a worksheet with questions to answer about the book we were reading, which was Lord of the Flies, by William Golding. I finished mine in good time, probably because I was quite intrigued by the story and had read and reread most of it. When I'd handed it in and gone back to my desk, I noticed that everyone else was still writing. So I sat and doodled in my planner, thinking about human nature. Actually, I was pondering William Golding's startling, brutal portrait of human nature. It was quite shocking to think that a group of civilised, well-educated boys could turn so primitive and savage. *Are we all harbouring the spirit of wild beasts?* I wondered uneasily.

"Right girls," Mrs Stokes' voice broke through my troubled thoughts.

"I spent the weekend going through your very enjoyable poems. And I must say I was very impressed. It was an exceedingly difficult job choosing just five to be read out on Friday. But Mrs Garnett insisted there'll only be time for five, so I've chosen Amanda Cartwright, Willow Wilkins, Layla Smith-Bailey, Hannah Wells, Beatrice Appleton-Ward and Eliza Dixon. Well done girls."

I could hardly contain my happiness! I had worked really hard on my poem and it had paid off! Even the daunting thought of reading it in front of hundreds of people couldn't dampen my enthusiasm.

The five of us met up with Mrs Stokes every day at lunchtime to practice reading our poems out loud with a microphone. We got more and more nervous as the days went by. Our art projects were on display in the grand foyer and everyone admired them as they passed. Miss Mason had decided to display all of them, as they had come out so well and there was more than enough room in the expansive foyer. By Thursday there was blue and purple bunting fluttering around the perimeter of the courtyard, as well as in the grand hall and foyer. Vases were positioned in various places, filled with stunning blue and purple lilies. Trophies were polished and everything gleamed.

Our usual homework session on Thursday evening was cancelled, and we were told to make sure our hair was washed and shining, and that fresh school uniform was put out for the next day. We also had to pack our bags for the Christmas holiday.

"And don't forget to polish your shoes!" Mrs Tupperley added sternly.

Friday dawned icy cold and clear, with a harsh, shimmering frost. We had a short assembly, in which Mrs Garnett went over the programme for the day and reminded us about the necessity for impeccable manners.

"Remember," she said, "you are all young ladies, and that is exactly how you should behave."

Parents and visitors started to arrive at ten, and by eleven everyone was gathered in the grand hall. It was a huge room with wood-panelled walls and massive chandeliers suspended from the high ceiling. As we took our seats, resplendent in our smart uniforms, I actually felt proud to be a student at Hilltop Hall. First we sang Over the Rainbow, from the musical The Wizard of Oz and then a special visitor gave a speech. She was a famous author who wrote books for teenagers, and as well as being really interesting, her talk had me seriously considering a future writing career for myself. When she'd finished, Mrs Garnett announced that some of us 'talented writers' had written wonderful poems and would be reading them out. I suddenly felt very nervous. Beatrice was the first up and she sounded really confident. Her poem was about the spirit of the horse, and how these marvellous creatures should be treated with love and respect. Everyone listened attentively and clapped politely and then it was my turn. My stomach did somersaults as I walked up the steps and onto the stage.

"Worlds Apart," I began, and then proceeded to recite my poem about two girls from totally different backgrounds who became best friends against all odds. After reading the first few lines I actually started to relax and enjoy myself. I really believed I'd written a good poem and it felt great to be sharing it with others. I think they must have enjoyed it too, because there was a lot of enthusiastic clapping as I made my way back to my seat. The other poems were read and then Mrs Garnett gave a speech about the history of the school. To end off, we all sang the school song. We stayed seated as the parents and visitors made their way out; then we went to get ready for the lunchtime banquet. I spotted Flo in the corridor just outside the grand hall.

"Lizzie!" she cried. "Are your mum and dad here?"

"No, my parents couldn't get time off work. My mum will be here this evening to pick me up though."

Flo threw her arms around me. "Oh Lizzie," she said warmly, "I loved your poem and I'm really going to miss you over Christmas!"

"I'm going to miss you too," I said. "But we'll be able to chat on the phone and online so it won't be too bad!"

Lunch was exceptional. There were so many decadent foods to choose from and the dining hall - with its candles, dainty napkins and beautiful china - looked fit for royalty. Everyone enjoyed themselves and the whole day looked like a huge success. The atmosphere was really festive, probably because the Christmas holiday was just around the corner.

When the celebrations were at last over, we went to our rooms to finish getting ready for the holidays. Mrs Stokes stopped me on my way out to congratulate me on my poem, which she said many of the visitors had been very impressed with. So, bursting with pride, I entered my room a few minutes later. Then my heart sank right down into my well-polished shoes. On my bed was my bag, packed and ready, but there was a note taped to it. In big assorted letters cut out randomly from a magazine, is said:

MISS DOOLITTLE

YOU DO NOT BELONG HERE

DON'T BOTHER COMING BACK

It felt good to be home, stretched out on my bed with a book and my cat, Thomas, cuddled up warm beside me. My mum had cooked a lovely meal to welcome me home and I didn't have the heart to tell her I was still nearly bursting from lunch. So I lay there uncomfortably, feeling like an overstuffed turkey. I couldn't concentrate on what I was reading; my mind kept travelling back to the note on my bag. I wondered whose idea it was. I thought it was probably Meredith's, but I suspected a few of her friends were also involved. Layla must have seen it, although she had already left when I got to our room. Thinking about those girls, I began to feel the anger and frustration welling up inside me all over again. Eventually I got up and went over to my computer, where I googled 'Magic Spells.'

Wow! I thought, gazing at the screen. *Over eight million hits!* I scrolled down the page, completely overwhelmed by the amount of information staring back at me. I didn't know where to start. I continued to gaze at the screen until a beep from my phone brought me back to reality. It was a text from Flo. It said: "Missing you! Snowing here, going sledging tomorrow. Will ring soon so we can catch up. Flo x." I smiled and thought how lucky I was to have made such a good friend.

The weekend dragged by and I was disappointed that we didn't have any snow. At least you could have fun in the snow, like sledging and building a snowman and things. But we only had rain and it was cold, grey and miserable. Some friends from my old school popped over on the Sunday and we watched a few DVDs together. It was fun and I felt my spirits start to lift a bit. On Monday morning I decided to walk into town. But I had to take my nine year old brother, George, along with me, because I was responsible for him while Mum and Dad were at work. It was so embarrassing having to drag him along with me, but I had no choice.

"Where are we going?" he asked irritably as we left the house. "I hope not shopping, you know I hate shopping!"

"Stop whining!" I snapped. "Do you think I like having to take you everywhere with me?"

We walked the rest of the way in silence. When we got into town I headed straight to the New Age shop, which had the wonderfully mysterious name of Edna's Esoteric Eden. George gave me a curious look as we entered but said nothing. But his eyes soon grew huge as he took in the extraordinary sight of all the strange and curious items. "Wow!" he said, looking impressed. "I've never been in here before! This place is so cool!" Then he added, "What's that stinky perfume smell?"

I ignored him and went to look at the books. I picked one up; it was called Necromancy. I wasn't even sure what that meant. Then I heard a friendly voice behind me.

"Hi there, I'm Edna. Is there anything I can help you with?"

"Uh, hi," I said, caught off guard. "I, um, I'm interested in, um, magic and um, spells."

Edna smiled knowingly and immediately put me at ease.

"Well," she said, turning to a nearby shelf, "if you're just starting out I would recommend this." She picked up a beautifully carved wooden box. "It's an excellent kit which contains a book as well as all the essential items to get you started."

She handed me the box and I turned it over in my hands. It was about the size of a shoebox, quite heavy and similar in shape to a traditional treasure chest. I thought it looked expensive. Luckily I still had my birthday money saved from August. I lifted the lid to have a look at the contents. I didn't recognise anything except for three candles, so I quickly closed it and said, "Thank you, I'll take it."

As soon as we were out of the shop, George looked up at me with an expectant grin.

"Well?" he asked inquisitively. "What did you buy? I mean I saw the box, but what's in it?"

"Look George," I said seriously, "I really don't want Mum and Dad to know about this. I don't think they'd like it. If I take you for a milkshake, will you promise not to say anything to them?"

"Hmmm," he said, grinning mischievously, "I have a counter proposal for you."

"Ha!" I spat with a laugh. "Do you even know what that means?"

"I won't tell Mum and Dad," he said slyly, "if you take me for a double chocolate milkshake and you let me see what's in the box."

I stopped dead in my tracks. I couldn't believe the boy! At his age, he had me between a rock and a hard place!

When we got home I took the box straight up to my room, set it down on my bed and opened it. George was right there, of course, barely able to contain his curiosity. He watched, wide-eyed, as I carefully unpacked each item. There were three candles: one pink, one white and one green. Each had a small piece of paper attached to it. The one on the pink candle said 'love, morality, honour;' the one on the white said 'truth, purity,' and the one on the green said 'money, luck, fertility.'

There was also a small candleholder, some incense, an incense holder, a selection of crystals in a purple velvet pouch, a brass pentacle, a small bag of sea salt and some natural oil. I was enthralled as I continued to unpack the box. Next I lifted out a glass bottle with a cork lid, labelled 'Spell bottle.' Then I found three bags of herbal mixes. The first was labelled 'To attract love', the next said 'For purification' and the last one said 'To attract money'. Then right at the bottom of the box were two books. The one was called Book of Spells and the other was filled with blank pages and had the name Book of Shadows in gold lettering on the front. Attached to that book with a little ribbon was a clear bag containing a quill pen and a jar of ink labelled 'Dragon's Blood ink.' When at last everything was spread out on my bed, I looked up for the first time and saw

George's mouth hanging open.

"Lizzy," he said nervously, "I've seen this kind of stuff on movies. It's fun to watch, but I don't think it's good to play around with it."

"Nah, you've just been watching the wrong kind of movies," I said, and then added, "Oh and don't forget our little agreement - or I might just use some of this stuff on you!

Christmas came and went and soon it was time to go back to school. George had been really good about keeping our secret, and I had read and reread the spell book and practiced magic whenever I was alone. I also printed tons of pages of notes off the internet. But despite all that, I still hadn't had any results - well nothing you could prove was really due to magic. I did do a money spell and then got some money for Christmas, but of course that might have had nothing to do with the spell.

CHAPTER 6

A HEX I PUT UPON YOU

The day I returned to school my head was pounding like a jackhammer and I felt out of sorts. Mum thought I might be coming down with something, but I knew it was the stress of going back to school that was causing it. For the last few days I'd been thinking about the note I'd found taped to my bag, and wondering what those awful girls might have planned for me this term.

As we drove through the school gates and Mum found parking on the gravel, I hoped no one was around to notice our ancient green rust bucket of a car. I was so embarrassed to be seen anywhere near it, especially with all the smart new cars (mostly four-by-fours) parked all around. So I hurriedly grabbed my bag from the boot, said a hasty goodbye to Mum, and made my way quickly into Atlee House. But I realised luck hadn't been on my side as I walked into my room and saw Layla looking out the window. She turned to me with a sneer.

"What were you doing in that hideous old green banger?" She asked in disgust.

I swallowed, trying to think of something to say.

"Um," I said, dropping my heavy bag, "we're just borrowing it while ours' is in the garage."

Layla sniggered and went to sort out her clothes. I knew she didn't believe me and I felt humiliated, so I left my bag on my bed and went to find Flo. I found her a few minutes later in Churchill House, making a cup of hot cocoa.

"Lizzie!" she cried when she saw me. "I'm so pleased to see you again! Would you like a mug of something hot? I'm trying to warm up; this place is freezing!"

"Sounds good," I said. "Thanks."

We were the only ones in the common room, so we sat down and made ourselves comfortable. We had a lot of catching up to do, and in the end I only returned to my room after supper that evening. It was dark when I opened the door, and I fumbled for the light switch. When at last the room was filled with light, and I had blinked a few times, I stood and stared in horror at the mess. My bag had been opened and my belongings lay strewn all over the floor. Then a feeling of dread washed over me as I noticed the wooden box. It was closed but the contents had been emptied out. I went over and opened the lid. Inside was a note scribbled in black marker. It said:

ELIZA D IS A WITCH

And underneath was a crude drawing of an ugly, pointy-nosed witch on a broomstick. I felt so violated. My cheeks flushed red as I felt a powerful anger rise up inside me. I hurriedly packed away the contents of the box and hid it under my bed. Then I packed away all my clothes and other belongings. While I worked, a plan was forming in my mind, and I hastily dug out the file I'd brought back with me, which contained all my printed notes on magic and spells. It was time to try some real magic.

The following day I collected everything I'd need, which involved sneaking into the conservatory to get some herbs. I needed a sprig of Hemlock and a Tormentil leaf. Flo stood watch for me and I made sure I was in and out faster than those bullies could say 'Eliza D is a witch.' After school, Flo came up to my room with me. Layla wasn't there, thank goodness, because I needed something of hers in order to make the spell work. I noticed her hairbrush lying on her dressing table, and quickly tugged some long brown hairs from it. Then I gathered everything else I'd need, and we made our way towards the woods, making sure no one spotted us.

It was a bitterly cold January day and nobody was out. Snow lay thick on the ground, the weak winter sun powerless to melt it. Everything looked bleak and colourless, and I noticed the pond was frozen solid.

When we reached a clearing in the woods, I opened the little bag I'd brought with. Pulling off my gloves, I put the candle, wand and bits of Layla's hair, along with the herbs and little bowl containing some Luck Oil, on a tree stump.

I knelt down and lit the candle, my hands shaking from the intense cold, before adding the dark green Tormentil leaf to the bowl. I'd read that Tormentil is a commanding herb which is often used to command respect, and works well with Hemlock, which is one of the best hexing agents. When Hemlock is combined with Luck Oil, it's supposed to change its meaning. So I combined the Hemlock with the other ingredients in the bowl and opened my Book of Shadows to the page where I'd written the spell. All this time Flo stood nearby, silently observing everything I did.

At last I held up my wand and said solemnly:

'You've done me wrong, now feel my wrath,

A hex I put upon you;

Nothing evil, just enough

To make you feel as I do.

So mote it be.'

Then I blew out the candle. Flo looked amused.

"Florence Knowles!" I scolded. "It isn't funny! This is very serious!"

"I know, I know!" she giggled. "You were just so theatrical! It was like watching a performance of the witches in Macbeth or maybe that scene in A Midsummer Night's Dream where Puck goes around casting spells with magic herbs. Really Lizzy, I think you'd do well to join the Speech and Drama Club!"

I ignored Flo and, with freezing fingers, poured the potion into my spell bottle, putting the cork tightly in the top. Now I just had to wait for something to happen.

***

I was feeling disheartened when, after three days, the spell had seemingly had no effect. I agonised over what I could have done wrong, but couldn't think of anything. I had taken great care with both the planning and the casting of the spell.

"I don't think my spell worked," I complained to Flo on Thursday during lunch.

"Maybe you did something wrong or left something out," she said.

"But I checked and double-checked. I'm sure I did everything right," I said, puzzled.

Then that evening, as everyone was getting ready to go down to supper, I heard a frightful shriek coming from the bathroom down the corridor. It sounded like Layla and I rushed to see what had happened.

"Layla?" I called, knocking on the bathroom door. "Is everything alright?"

"Aaaaaarrrrrgggggghhhhhh!" she continued to scream.

Then the door flew open and she appeared, red-faced and fuming.

"What are you staring at?" she screeched.

And then I saw it - bright red and shining magnificently like a lighthouse beacon. It took all my self-control not to start jumping up and down with joy and singing a song of triumph as I marvelled at the enormous pimple on the end of Layla's nose. She was obviously distraught and ran down the hallway in tears.

Layla skipped supper that evening, and I found her lying on her bed when I got back up to our room. As I entered, she turned and looked at me with intense loathing.

"You nasty little witch!" she snarled. "I bet you're enjoying this!"

I looked at her blankly. "I don't know what you're talking about," I said innocently, as I started getting ready for bed.

The next day there was a lot of whispering and snickering in the corridors. Layla was wearing a plaster on her nose, and telling everyone who would listen that she had been hit in the face during hockey practice. Flo was impressed. She admitted she hadn't really thought the spell would work, but now felt fairly certain we could take this as a positive result.

The next few days passed without incident. Layla wasn't speaking to me, but I didn't care. She spent most of her time out of our room, which suited me perfectly, because it meant I had time to read about and practice magic. The weather was atrocious anyway, with blizzard-like conditions, so we were more or less stuck indoors. Then by the end of the week I became aware of people giving me strange looks. *Maybe I'm just being paranoid,* I thought.

But then Flo called me aside at lunch and said, "Lizzy, there's a rumour going around that you're a witch. I'm sure you can guess who started it."

So that's why people are giving me odd looks, I thought.

***

On Friday after school, two girls I barely knew came up to me. One of them said, "Eliza? Uh, I don't think we've met. My name's Seren Bagrin and this is my friend Hannah Wells."

"Hi," said Hannah shyly.

"Uh, hi," I said uncertainly.

"We'd really like to talk to you," said Seren hesitantly. "Somewhere private."

I suggested we go to the library, which was usually quiet on Friday afternoons. The large room was silent except for the echo of our footsteps as we made our way over to the comfortable sofa at the far end. As we sat, I looked from Hannah to Seren and wondered what this could possibly be about. Seren was a tiny girl, like a little elf. She had shoulder length, almost black hair and the strangest eyes. The irises were so pale as to be almost colourless, and surrounded by a dark blue outer ring. I couldn't stop looking at them; they were almost luminescent, like the moon. There was definitely a mysterious quality about Seren, making it difficult to form a reliable first impression.

In contrast, Hannah was a slim girl of average height with long, straight brown hair, hazel eyes and high, prominent cheekbones. She seemed like a quiet, shy girl, and it was obvious she worshipped the ground Seren walked on.

"Look, I don't know how to say this," began Seren, "but we heard a rumour and were wondering if it was true."

"Oh!" I said wryly. "So that's what this is about."

"No, no," Hannah interjected, looking worried. "It's not what you think. You see…" her voice trailed off.

"What she's trying to say," said Seren, "is that we also, you know, dabble a bit in magic."

***

"Where on earth have you been?" demanded Flo, running her had through her hair in exasperation.

"Sorry!" I said, and proceeded to tell her all about my fascinating meeting with Hannah and Seren.

She looked thoughtful for a minute.

"You know," she said at last, "I always thought there was something, er, different about those two."

"They suggested the four of us meet up somewhere this weekend. Seren said it's best to meet at night, under cover of darkness."

Flo narrowed her eyes suspiciously. "Under cover of darkness? Why? They're not into anything illegal, are they?"

"Oh Flo!" I laughed. "You can be hilarious sometimes!"

CHAPTER 7

SISTERS OF THE CRAFT

We would have liked to meet up in the woods, but it was far too cold to venture out there in the middle of the night. So we were delighted when Seren remembered an old attic room which she and Hannah had discovered while exploring the main school building one night.

I was terribly worried that Layla would wake up and catch me sneaking out. I also imagined Mrs Tupperley had super-acute hearing, but all seemed quiet and still when I met up with Seren in the common room. She also stayed in Attlee House, and we made our way out cautiously together. I had slipped my phone in my pocket, as it had a built-in torch which I thought might come in handy. Once outside, we hurried over to the main building and in through a side door which was never locked. It was a small but heavy wooden door, with one of those huge keyholes which you only see in very old buildings. I thought the key had probably been lost a long time ago and was now too out-dated to be replaced.

Once inside, we spotted Flo and Hannah waiting for us in the foyer. Being very old, the building has a labyrinth of narrow staircases in addition to the large and elegant main ones. A teacher had told us that these back staircases would have been used by the servants when the school was a grand country house in the olden days. They were like a maze and I hoped we wouldn't get lost, because they seemed incredibly spooky and very cold. They were also full of cobwebs that tickled our faces as we made our way in the dim light of my phone torch. But we continued on, eventually reaching a little landing which felt colder than any other place we'd been so far that night. It was an odd feeling; in fact, it was so strangely icy that I felt the hairs on the back of my neck stand up. Then Seren, who was leading the way, stopped abruptly and turned to face us.

"Wait guys!" she hissed, holding up her hand. "I'm sensing something."

We stopped and waited, and I wondered what she was on about. I hoped the house mistresses weren't coming after us.

"There's a young girl here," said Seren, staring straight ahead with a serious expression on her face. Confused, I turned and looked around but could only see the four of us.

"She was a servant in this house," Seren went on, "but she died right here, on this landing. I can see an image of her dropping something, maybe a tray, as she falls down the stairs."

I was stunned. It seemed Seren could see dead people. Wow. Hannah didn't look at all surprised, and declared that she could also feel something. Flo stood wide-eyed, looking paler than usual, which was very pale indeed. The whole incident lasted only a few minutes, and we were soon on our way again. Then it wasn't long before a steep, narrow, creaky wooden staircase led us up to the attic. Hannah flicked a switch and a single bare bulb lit up, casting a murky light on the dusty old room. I looked around at the assortment of items that had seemingly been dumped randomly about the place. There was a big antique cupboard standing next to some modern plastic chairs, a metal fold-out table and a number of cardboard boxes. Two old school desks (with angry-looking gouge marks on their surfaces) and a very warn and faded Persian rug completed the eclectic décor. Surprisingly, it wasn't all that cold up in the attic. *Maybe the warm air from the building rises up into here,* I thought abstractly as Hannah and Seren dragged the rug into the middle of the room.

We all sat down in a cloud of dust and Seren began to tell us her ideas for our little group. She suggested we form a 'coven,' which she explained was a group of people who practiced witchcraft. She said there were usually thirteen people in a coven, but that four would have to do. Then she asked if we were all in agreement, as she said she felt it was important that we made the decision of our own free will about whether or not we wanted to be initiated into the coven. It sounded quite exciting and we all agreed enthusiastically.

"Alright then," said Seren, looking pleased. "We'll have the initiation here tomorrow at midnight. Hannah and I will sneak up here during the day with all the stuff we'll need."

We went on talking for about an hour, mainly asking Seren questions about what she called her 'gift'. She said she'd always been able to see and communicate with spirits of the dead, and that it was just normal for her. Hannah said she was also trying to develop her psychic abilities. And although they were both very much into magic, Seren had been practicing for much longer than Hannah. I told them about the problems I'd had with Layla and Meredith and the other girls, and about how we thought Miss Angelica was a witch. Hannah and Seren looked at each other and smiled.

"I agree with you about Meredith and her chums," said Seren. "They're a bunch of stuck-up brats, especially that Layla. But as for Miss Angelica, Hannah and I are convinced she's just a harmless hedge witch. You know: a lone witch who is more into the green arts, herbal cures and healing spells. A practitioner of natural magic. They use nature's gifts of flowers, plants and herbs for medicinal and magical purposes. They make brews and potions and perform magical rituals and spells for the benefit of themselves and others - with harm to none. But don't worry," she added with a broad grin, "we'll show you what real witches do!"

Flo and I met at lunch the following day, which was Sunday. I was exhausted after the previous night's escapades and had only woken at half past ten. Bleary-eyed, I took my seat next to Flo at the table. I noticed she looked a bit worn-out, like she hadn't slept.

"What's wrong?" I whispered. "You look a bit worse for wear today."

"I couldn't sleep a wink," she said glumly.

"Well you'll have to sleep this afternoon or you won't be able to keep your eyes open tonight," I said, feeling a surge of excited anticipation about the night ahead.

Flo looked down at the untouched chicken salad on her plate. "I don't even know if I want to go tonight," she said quietly.

"What? I don't believe you Flo! Why don't you want to do this?"

She looked at me and I could see the worry in her eyes. "I just think maybe we're getting ourselves into something risky here. I don't know if we should be doing this. I'm a bit uncomfortable with it, that's all."

I had a lot of respect for Flo, but she could be such a party pooper at times. She'd seemed fine last night, though, so I couldn't believe her sudden change in attitude.

"Look," I said persuasively, "we don't really know what's going to happen tonight, but I'm sure we'll have a good time, regardless. So why don't you just come and see, and then you can make up your mind."

"Well I'll think about it," she said at last.

***

It felt so deliciously thrilling to be sneaking out in the middle of the night! I'd never done anything like it before the previous night, and thought for a moment about what a goody two-shoes I'd always been. Well, I mused, people change.

I was relieved to meet Flo on my way up to the attic. She didn't look happy, but at least she'd decided to come. Hannah and Seren were already there, setting things up on a make-shift altar which appeared to be the metal fold-out table covered with a white cloth. I was now familiar with most of the items on the altar. In addition to the usual things, there was a dish of what looked like oil, a bowl of water and one of salt, a red length of cord and a slightly dangerous-looking miniature sword. I noticed Flo looked anxious as she surveyed the altar. Then when everything was set out, Seren looked up and smiled.

"Right," she said, "everything's set. I'll just get our robes."

Flo glanced at me as Seren went over to the old cupboard and took out what she referred to as our 'robes.' In actual fact, they looked like nothing more than regular bed sheets with holes cut in the middle for our heads to stick through. Then I noticed that a pentagram had been drawn on the front of each one with a black marker. As Seren slipped the robes over our heads, I thought how comical we must look, but I didn't laugh because Hannah and Seren both looked awfully serious. Once we were 'appropriately' dressed, Hannah turned to us.

"The priestess requests that you wait outside," she said solemnly, promptly ushering us out of the attic.

Flo looked at me with raised eyebrows and I had to bite my lip to stop myself from giggling. Then Hannah went back in and closed the door and Flo and I sat down on the wooden steps to wait.

"Look at us," said Flo, holding out her robe. "I feel as if we're waiting backstage, about to go and perform some ludicrous play."

The combination of her words coupled with the image of how ridiculous we must look sent us both into fits of hysterical giggles. We had just managed to calm down when we heard a bell ring. Then the door opened and Hannah escorted us back into the room. She handed us scrolls which appeared to be scripts with responses to questions written on them. Seren stood behind the altar, and Hannah went to stand by her side. They both looked very solemn. Then Seren spoke.

"Eliza," she said authoritatively, "why do you come here?"

Hannah gestured to my script and I looked at the first response.

"Um, to worship the Gods in whom I believe and to become one with them and with my sisters in the Craft." I answered. This was repeated for Flo. Then we were told to respond in unison to all further questions. In script form, this is how it went:

Seren: What do you bring with you?

Flo and me: I bring nothing but my true self.

Seren: Then I bid you enter this, our circle of worship and magic. (Hannah then guided us into a circle which had been made with the red cord, and I noticed Seren pouring the salt into the bowl of water, before moving around the altar and coming to stand in front of us.)

Seren: To enter this, our sacred circle, I here duly consecrate you in the names of the God and the Goddess. (She then proceeded to sprinkle us with the salty water while Hannah rang the bell twice.)

Seren: Why are you here?

Flo and me: I am here to become one with the Lord and Lady; to join in worship of them.

Seren: Who made you come here?

Flo and me: (With Flo giving me a quick sideways glance) None made me come, for I am here of my own choosing.

Seren: Do you wish an end to the life you have known so far?

Flo and me: (A bit hesitantly) I do.

Seren: Then so be it.

(And with that, Hannah handed Seren the blade, with which she proceeded to cut off a small lock of each of our hair! Going to stand behind the altar again, Seren then placed a gold plastic crown on her head. Hannah went to stand next to her and rang the bell three times.)

Flo and I (Prompted by Hannah): I salute the Lord and the Lady, as I salute those who represent them. I pledge my love and support to them and to my sisters of the Craft.

Seren (holding up the bowl of oil): With this Sacred Oil I anoint and cleanse thee, giving new life to these Children of the Gods. So Mote It Be.

Hannah, Flo and me: So Mote It Be.

Seren: Now you are truly one of us. As one of us will you share our knowledge of the Gods and of the arts of divination, of magic and of

all the mystic arts. These shall you learn as you progress.
(Hannah then rang the bell three times.)

Seren: Now it is time for celebration!

Hannah went over to the old cupboard and returned with some plates of biscuits, a bag of crisps and some juice. I must say I really didn't feel like eating at one o'clock in the morning, but I didn't want to seem rude, so I had a biscuit and a cup of orange juice. Flo seemed to feel the same way as me. We sat around and talked for a while, but we had school in the morning, and we were tired, so we didn't stay long. It had been a very strange night. Well actually, it had been a very strange weekend, and I was glad to finally fall into bed, too exhausted to give the recent events much thought.

CHAPTER 8
ALL THINGS BLACK

The next few weeks were packed with exams, so there wasn't much time for magic. But the four of us did manage to meet in the attic every other Saturday night, and we always sat together at lunch time. Seren was teaching us all about 'Moon Magic.' She told us that the Moon is the most important heavenly body to witches. She said we draw on her power for lunar magic and cast our spells in accordance with her cycles. Seren said the Moon inspires and illuminates us. Even Flo admitted it was all very interesting.

Then just before the Easter holidays, when all our exams were finished, I remembered I still had the book Miss Angelica had lent us. So on Saturday morning Flo and I set off through the woods towards Cliodhna Cottage. The air was fresh and the first daffodils of spring were beginning to open in the sun.

"I love it when everything comes alive again," said Flo, twirling around like a contented little child.

"I know!" I said happily. "I can't wait for summer."

Miss Angelica was pleased to see us again, and asked if we'd found the book helpful.

"Oh yes," I said, "it was very informative. We learned a lot, thank you."

"And do you have any questions?" asked Miss Angelica kindly. "I'm sure there must have been quite a lot of information that was unfamiliar to you girls. I can honestly say it's taken me many, many years of study and practice to get to where I am today."

Flo and I looked at each other, not sure how to respond. We were very fond of Miss Angelica, but we'd agreed we wouldn't tell anyone about the magic coven. Seren had talked us into making a pact which she said must never be broken.

"Well," I said after a moment's pause, "during the Christmas holidays I visited a New Age shop in the town where I live. The lady who owns it was very helpful and sold me a really beautiful magic kit. It came with a book and some herbs and other things for spells, and I've been playing around with it a bit."

Miss Angelica looked thoughtful. "Just remember to be careful," she said earnestly. "Being a witch takes a lot of effort, study and responsibility. And always follow the code of ethics: Harm none, do as you will."

After enjoying some herbal tea and biscuits, Flo and I set off back to school. The sky had clouded over and it looked like we were in for some rain.

"So much for a nice sunny day," said Flo disappointedly.

***

When I got back to my room, I noticed that Layla wasn't there and all her things were gone. Just as I was thinking about how lovely it would be to have the place to myself, Willow popped her head through the door.

She was grinning broadly and said, "If you're wondering where Layla is, she's gone to see a derma-something-or-other doctor about that humungous zit on her nose. Oh and I heard she asked to be moved to a different room - said she couldn't be expected to live with a peasant."

***

The next few days flew by and soon it was the last day of Spring term. Flo's mum came to pick us both up so I could spend a few days with them. They lived in a small village, quiet and postcard-pretty with only one little shop. Nothing much happened around there, but luckily Flo's sister - who was nineteen and had a car – offered to drive us to a nearby beach where we had a super time. I still practiced magic whenever I had the chance, and when I got home George was eager to know what spells I had tried and if they had worked.

"Have you turned anyone into a frog yet?" he asked enthusiastically.

"Don't be ridiculous George," I said haughtily. "Spells like that are just pretend. My friends and I do real magic."

"Well then show me some real magic," he said. "Please!"

I thought for a moment and then said, "Okay, I'll show you a new one I've been practicing. But remember it's strictly between us."

"Cool!" said George, grinning from ear to ear like a loon.

Retrieving my wooden magic box from under my bed, I took out a small clear crystal and placed it on my dressing table.

"This is a teleportation spell," I said. "My friend Seren taught it to me. Teleportation is when you move an object using psychic power, or a kind of energy that comes from your mind, called telekinetic energy. It takes a lot of practice to be able to do it."

Taking a few deep breaths, I cleared my mind of all thoughts and held my hands out above the crystal, with my thumbs and index fingers touching to form a triangle. This is supposed to represent imagination, visualization, and will. I then closed my eyes and pictured the crystal moving, and while doing so, said, "Obiectum moveat!" Those are Latin words meaning to move an object.

I heard George's startled voice before I even opened my eyes. "Awesome!" he said in amazement. "One minute it was sitting there on your dresser, like a regular old stone, then I just blinked my eyes and it was gone! Where did it go?"

"I'm not sure," I said, trying to act cool but feeling insanely pleased that something had actually happened. "We'll have to look for it; I suppose it could be anywhere."

George and I searched my room, turning the place upside down and leaving a trail of stuffed animals and related disorder behind us. Then just as we were about to give up, I spotted the crystal glinting in the sun on the windowsill beside my dressing table. George was super-impressed and asked me to do some more spells for him.

"Maybe some other time," I said. "Spells use up a lot of energy and I have to concentrate so hard it feels like my brain's about to burst."

***

The holidays passed far too quickly, and soon it was time to return to school.

"Mum, please drop me off just outside the gates," I said as we approached the entrance.

"Lizzy why would you want me to do that?" asked Mum, frowning.

"Um, I could do with a good walk in the fresh air," I said unconvincingly.

"Nonsense!" said Mum. "All the other parents drive their children right into school. And you've got that heavy bag to carry."

I cringed as Mum drove right up to the entrance of Attlee House in our old green rattletrap. And to make matters worse, the horrid thing had developed a hole in its exhaust, causing it to make even more noise than usual and attracting an increasing number of shocked stares. Blushing with embarrassment, I said a quick goodbye, grabbed my bag and hurried into school. *Please don't let anyone have noticed me,* I thought self-consciously.

I found Flo and Seren waiting for me in the Attlee House foyer. We hugged and said our hellos before the two of them followed me up to my room. We were chatting away happily when I opened the door, then suddenly we all stopped dead in our tracks and stared in disbelief. Someone had obviously been very busy in my room. One of the walls had been painted black and I could still smell the fresh paint. Then there was what looked like ketchup dripping down two of the other walls. There were also plastic spiders stuck here and there in those phoney spider webs that people put up at Halloween. But what really horrified me was the dead bat which hung above my desk. The nauseating stench emanating from it left me in no doubt that it was the real thing.

In complete shock, I turned and looked at my friends who were standing wide-eyed in the doorway. Flo was the first to speak.

"Let's help you get this place cleaned up," she said, taking charge of the situation.

"And don't worry about the bat," said Seren. "I'll take care of that."

We cleaned up as best we could, but I was terrified Mrs Tupperley would find out about it. There were a few days left 'til room inspection, and I intended to find some white paint and cover the black wall as soon as possible. But as it turned out, I wasn't so lucky. The following day before school, there was a knock at my door.

"Come in!" I called, frantically brushing my hair.

The door opened and there stood the colossal Mrs Tupperley, out of breath and wheezing slightly. She was holding one of my school books.

"Eliza, you shouldn't leave your books lying in the hallway! A person could slip and…" Her voice trailed off as her eyes settled on the black wall.

"What," she boomed, "is that?"

Oh I was in such big trouble.

***

Four high-backed wooden chairs stood along the wall outside Mrs Garnett's office. This area was called the 'Corridor of Doom,' because if you found yourself sitting on one of those chairs, you knew you were in serious trouble.

I waited nervously for what seemed like ages while Mrs Garnett was busy taking assembly. When she eventually appeared, she ignored me completely, went inside her office, and shut the door. About twenty minutes later the door opened and she called me in, gesturing for me to take a seat in a big leather chair in front of her vast mahogany desk. Everything was silent and I could feel a knot forming in my stomach. Mrs Garnett looked particularly stern, her mouth set in a grim line.

"Miss Dixon," she began, "we take waywardness and misbehaviour very seriously at Hilltop Hall. I am aware that this is your first misdemeanour; however, it is a very grave one. When we say you may personalise your room, what we mean is your choice of soft furnishings, ornaments, pictures, et cetera. What you did is equivalent to vandalism."

I looked at Mrs Garnett in disbelief - she just assumed I was guilty! I opened my mouth to speak, but she silenced me by raising her index finger and shaking her head. She wasn't even giving me the chance to explain to her that I didn't do it. *It's so unfair!* I thought angrily.

"You will have detention every Friday afternoon for the rest of this term," Mrs Garnett continued unemotionally. "Dismissed."

Tears stung my eyes as I made my way to the cloakroom. I couldn't believe the injustice! Making my way into one of the empty stalls, I sank to the floor with my head in my hands and cried. I don't know how much time passed, but after a while I began to feel different. Like a determined little chick resolutely pecking itself out of its egg shell, I stopped feeling sorry for myself as an iron will rose up inside me, replacing all feelings of despondency. *I'll get my revenge!* I thought resolutely. *And when I do I swear it's going to be wicked!*

CHAPTER 9

THE HORSE WHISPERER

It had been a difficult week. Not only did I have to sit through detention on Friday afternoon, but I also had to spend my entire Saturday morning painting the wall in my room. And it needed several coats to properly cover the black. By midday I was bored and in a bad mood, but at least my room was back to normal. I cleaned myself up and went down to lunch, taking my place between Hannah and Flo. They looked at me sympathetically.

"Sorry you had to do it all by yourself," Flo said kindly. "You know we would've helped if we'd been allowed."

"I know," I said. "But its ok, I got it all done."

"Seren said she feels like a walk this afternoon," said Hannah. "She wondered if we'd all like to go."

"Well I could definitely do with some fresh air after all those stinky paint fumes!" I said. "And the weather's super."

So after lunch we set off for our walk. It was warm and sunny out and I soon began to feel better. Seren led the way down past the sports fields and through a little meadow. It looked so pretty with all the wild flowers and beautiful clumps of daffodils under the trees.

The birds chirped and it became so warm that we stopped to take off our jumpers. Then we continued over a little wooden bridge which led us over a crystal clear stream at the bottom of the meadow. Continuing on the grassy path, we soon found ourselves at the far end of the stables, where the paddocks were.

I had never been down to that area of the property and was just thinking how lovely it was, when we became aware of some commotion behind a nearby hedge. There was a lot of shouting and the sound of a horse's hooves scrabbling frantically on the ground. So with our curiosity aroused, we went to find out what was going on. As soon as we rounded the hedge we saw Meredith, Layla, Beatrice, Cassie and Amanda staring at a big grey horse which was snorting and rolling its eyes while frantically pawing the ground with one of its hooves.

"I'm not going back in there!" Cassie screamed at Meredith. "He nearly killed me that time!"

"Oh come on!" Meredith said venomously. "You're such a little wimp! I'll show you how it's done!"

And with that, she ducked under one of the wooden fence poles and into the circular paddock. The horse snorted loudly, the whites of his eyes showing as he tossed his head agitatedly. Meredith approached slowly, reaching out her arm to try and take hold of the head collar. But the horse looked panicked and suddenly took off galloping around the paddock, kicking up his legs in a tempestuous shower of thick dust as Meredith quickly escaped under one of the fence poles. "Damn!" she said irritably. "I almost had him."

"Just leave him in there for tonight," said Layla.

"And don't give him anything to eat," added Amanda. "That'll teach him."

Just then Meredith noticed us standing by the hedge. "What are you weirdoes staring at?" she shouted rudely, before turning and heading back to the stables. The other girls immediately turned and followed her.

"Wow," said Seren in awe, looking over at the big grey horse. "He's so beautiful."

"And crazy by the looks of things," I said.

Seren wandered over to the paddock, looking mesmerised, and we all followed. The horse was now standing at the far end of the paddock, sweating profusely and breathing heavily.

"No, he's not crazy," she said matter-of-factly. "Just misunderstood."

And without another word she ducked under the fence, just as Meredith had done, and walked calmly over to the horse, which was eyeing her suspiciously. We watched with interest as Seren placed her hands behind her back, closed her eyes, and blew into the horse's nostrils. His ears immediately pricked forward and he visibly relaxed. Then she opened her eyes and lifted her right arm quickly, which sent the horse trotting away from her. She kept chasing him around in a circle, while gently encouraging him with her voice. This all went on for some time, until eventually – while still trotting around - the horse lowered his head and it looked like he was chewing something. I didn't understand what was happening but it was all so intriguing that I found I couldn't look away for a second.

Eventually Seren put both her arms against her sides and looked down at the ground. She didn't say or do anything, but the horse stopped trotting, turned and walked slowly but steadily towards her. He stopped right in front of her, standing quietly with his head down as Seren proceeded to run her hands all over his body. It seemed unbelievable that this was the same wild, agitated animal we'd been watching just half an hour ago, and the three of us continued to look on in silence. Then all of a sudden Seren reached up and took hold of the purple head collar. Then she turned and led the horse over to the fence where she climbed onto one of the poles and carefully positioned herself across the horse's back. Hannah, Flo and I stared in awe at the miracle unfolding in front of us. The horse stood perfectly still, and after a few minutes Seren threw her right leg carefully over his back until she was sitting astride him. Then very slowly, she encouraged him to move forward as she held onto a handful of his mane. The big horse walked serenely around the paddock, and after a few minutes Seren asked if one of us would open the gate for her.

Hannah rushed over to open it, and Seren told us to follow her to the stables. Of course we did just that and were soon treated to some of the most shocked expressions I've ever had the pleasure of witnessing in my entire life. The five girls' mouths dropped open and for once they were rendered speechless. Cassie was the first to find her voice.

"What are you doing on my horse?" she squawked.

"What does it look like I'm doing?" asked Seren with a deadpan expression.

"How did you…" Amanda began, "I mean, he hasn't even been broken in yet."

Seren swung gracefully down off the horse's back. "Well he has now," she said simply.

***

The three of us had a newfound respect for Seren after the horse incident. Believing that she could communicate with animals using her psychic powers, we felt she was quite an extraordinary person indeed, and we all sort of looked up to her. And of course Hannah now worshipped her more than ever. Then a few days later, while we were sitting outside enjoying the spring sunshine, Flo suggested we think of a name for the group that consisted of Meredith and her friends.

"I know!" Hannah piped up quickly. "We could call them the 'Toffees' because they're so stuck-up and toffee-nosed!"

"Hey that's brilliant!" said Flo, and we all agreed.

Meanwhile, I was enjoying having Seren as a roommate. I'll admit she was a bit eccentric in her ways, but she was easy enough to get on with and at least we didn't have to worry about hiding our magic. She was teaching me a lot and we had recently started meditating together nearly every day. Seren believed meditation was the backbone of any spell casting and magic work, and said if you lack the skills to meditate and to hold a single thought in your mind for at least 10 minutes, you will have a very hard time having success in spell casting. So most mornings we got up extra early to meditate. It was quite hard at first but I eventually got the hang of it. We sat cross-legged on the rug between our beds, lit a candle, and then stared at the burning flame for about fifteen minutes. During that time, we had to empty our minds and think of nothing - just focus on the flame. But it wasn't as easy as it sounds! Thoughts kept trying to get into my head! When I looked at Seren, she seemed to almost be in a trance, like her body was there, but her mind or spirit was somewhere else. It was quite creepy sometimes.

The Toffees seemed to dislike not only me, but my friends as well. I think it had a lot to do with the horse incident. They must have thought we'd got the better of them or something. And that's probably what led to their next sneaky trick.

CHAPTER 10

CRICKETS

We were allowed into town on the first Saturday of every month, but I had only started going since Flo and I became friends. We had to go in full school uniform, which was a bit of a drag, but we all looked forward to it as it got us off the school property for a day. Most of the girls used it as an opportunity to meet up with boys from the local school. Well it was our only opportunity to mix with members of the opposite sex! So with our free Saturday only days away, it was all we could talk about. None of us had a boyfriend except Seren, who was in love with a local boy who had dropped out of school. His name was Dylan and he was training to be a mechanic. Seren said her parents would never approve of the relationship. But she smiled when she said it - like she was pleased she was doing something they wouldn't agree with.

When Saturday eventually came round, and I'd survived another tedious Friday afternoon detention, we all got out our carefully hidden make-up and did up our faces. Some girls waited until they got into town before doing themselves up, because they were afraid of getting caught and banned from going out. But we all waited until we were almost in town before hitching our skirts up a few inches higher, taking off our hats and ties, and undoing the top few buttons of our shirts. It felt so exciting to be free and rebelling against what we considered to be very inconsiderate school rules. I mean how were we supposed to attract boys while wearing straw boater hats, below-the-knee skirts and shirts buttoned up to our throats?

We spotted Dylan leaning against the bridge on the way into town. He had on ripped jeans, a leather jacket and trainers, and was smoking a cigarette. Seren ran straight up to him and they kissed passionately. Then he lit another cigarette and handed it to her. I said 'hi' to him, but he just nodded and looked away. Seren had told us he was very quiet and didn't say much. She also said he was very misunderstood. But I could certainly see why she was attracted to him. He was terribly good looking in a troubled, brooding sort of way – a bit like a twenty-first century James Dean.

We left the two of them together and wandered down towards the marketplace. The choice of shops was quite limited in the old cobbled town. Altogether, there were two banks, a hair salon, a pet shop, a small supermarket, a charity shop, an expensive country clothing store, a pharmacy, a café, two gift shops and a couple of pubs. There was a chilly wind blowing and we wanted to be inside somewhere warm, so we went into the charity shop and had fun trying on all the fancy prom dresses, hats and high heeled shoes. We posed and took photos with our phone cameras, laughing and talking happily until we stepped out the door and came face-to-face with the Toffees, who happened to be walking past. And they weren't on their own - they were with a group of gorgeous, well-dressed boys.

"Hey, look!" Meredith said loudly. "It's those loser freaks doing their shopping! And how appropriate for them to be buying from the local charity shop!"

She put a lot of emphasis on the last two words, and the others stared at us and laughed openly. It was so humiliating and we were so taken by surprise that we couldn't think of anything clever to say back to them.

"I am so going to even the score one of these days," I said angrily, as the Toffees walked off self-importantly, with the boys following close behind.

"You're not the only one," said Hannah in disgust.

We had a look around for Seren and Dylan but couldn't find them anywhere, so we went and had some lunch at the café. It was warm and cosy inside, and we managed to find a table at one of the front windows, so we could look out and see who was doing what. The café was right in the middle of the square, so we were well-placed to see what was going on.

"Look!" said Flo conspiratorially when we'd ordered our food. "There's Willow holding hands with that boy who was going out with Cassie! They must have broken up!"

"And look there!" I said, craning my neck and pointing to the pet shop straight across from the window where we sat. "The Toffees are going into the pet shop!"

"That's odd," said Hannah, frowning. "Everyone knows we're not allowed to keep pets at school."

"Maybe they're going to buy horsey things," said Flo.

"I've never seen anything remotely horsey in there," said Hannah thoughtfully. Then she turned to us with a huge grin. "Hey, have you guys seen the weird old woman with the shaggy grey hair who works there? The one with hundreds of little ratty-looking dogs."

"No," I said. "Flo and I have never been in there."

"Well she has a son," Hannah went on. "He goes to the local high school. Do you know what his name is?" We looked at her in expectation.

"Jack," she said, grinning widely. "Second name Russell - like the dogs!"

"Poor kid," said Flo sympathetically.

And with that we all burst into fits of laughter, forgetting all about the Toffees and their visit to the pet shop.

After lunch we found Seren and Dylan sitting on a bench beside the river. Seren's head was resting on Dylan's shoulder and the two of them looked totally loved up. Seren's hair was tussled and her clothes looked all crumpled, and Flo gave me a nudge and a look as if to say, I wonder what they've been up to! We stood and waited for them to bid each other a long and drawn-out goodbye, which was looking more and more like a scene from some romantic tragedy, in which the lovers aren't sure if they'll ever see each other again. Then, with hats and ties replaced and skirts pulled down to their usual length, we began our walk back up the steep hill to school.

As Seren and I approached our room, she yawned and said, "I'm going straight to bed. Don't bother waking me for supper; I'm not hungry."

I thought briefly about how moody she could be sometimes, but I said okay and opened the door to our room.

"Oh what fresh hell is this?" I squealed with a shudder as I surveyed the scuttling black mass of insects which obscured the entire floor of our bedroom. "So that's what they were doing in the pet shop."

"What are you talking about?" shrieked Seren. "Were the hell did all these crickets come from?"

I told her how we'd seen the Toffees going into the pet shop at lunch time, and that I was sure that probably explained our present situation. Seren was silent as her face took on a downright malevolent look. I actually felt scared.

"I am going to make sure those snotty, conceited little brats get exactly what they deserve," she said very slowly and deliberately, as we continued to survey the chaos from the doorway.

With their hard black bodies, spiky legs and long antennae, the crickets gave me the absolute creeps. Seren and I tiptoed into the room, being careful not to stand on them, then quickly jumped up onto our beds. The crickets made a constant chirping noise which was enough to drive a person mad, and I wondered how on earth we were going to get rid of them. There was certainly no way I was going to touch the hideous-looking creatures. But luckily Seren quickly came up with a plan.

"You know," she said contemplatively, as we sat perched on our beds, "we can also play this game. But for now, I know of a spell that should dispose of these annoying little blighters."

Then I watched, intrigued, as she tip-toed over to her cupboard and extracted her smart birch wood wand from under a pile of jumpers. Then she opened the window wide before closing her eyes and becoming very still. Suddenly she waved the wand in a swift, well-practiced circular movement and exclaimed, "Eradico!"

All of a sudden the crickets formed a dense black cloud as they rose as one toward the open window and disappeared into the gathering dusk. When they'd all gone, Seren promptly closed the window, looking pleased with herself.

"A simple banishing spell," she said dismissively. "Well at least now I'll be able to get some sleep." Then she added, "I think we should keep quiet about this. Pretend like there were never any crickets here. Don't give those Toffees the satisfaction of thinking they got us."

We only told Hannah and Flo about the crickets. They were shocked and approved of our idea to come up with a plan for revenge. Saturday night would be our meeting in the attic, and we all agreed to give it some thought before then. But in the meantime, the week seemed to drag on and on. By the time Friday came I couldn't wait for the weekend. Our last lesson of the day was Herbology, but I still had detention after that, which made me feel irritable and annoyed. Miss Angelica sailed into the classroom, her long summery dress floating gracefully around her like the wings of a butterfly on a gentle breeze. She always seemed so full of energy and vitality, drawing us all effortlessly into her lessons with her captivating enthusiasm. That particular lesson turned out to be really enjoyable and just what I needed at the end of a difficult week.

"I thought we'd do something a bit different today," Miss Angelica said, smiling. "So we're going to make bath bombs! You know - those lovely fragranced balls which dissolve in your bath and are simply heavenly after a tiring day. Oh how I love to lie in a bath with some herbal bath bombs, a candle and a good book!"

She called us up to a long wooden table where she'd set out all the ingredients. There was bicarbonate of soda, citric acid, some oil, food colouring, a few bottles of essential oils made from plants, and some dried lavender and rose petals. Miss Angelica began by explaining the chemical reaction between the main ingredients, which takes place in the water and creates the fizzing bubbles. She then told us to choose which essential oils we'd like to use, based on our knowledge of their properties.

It was great fun making bath bombs! We mixed all the ingredients together, added petals for decoration, and then put them in moulds to set. Miss Angelica said they'd be ready to collect at our next Herbology lesson. While we were busy cleaning up and packing everything away, Miss Angelica came over and quietly asked me to stay for a few minutes after the lesson. I was puzzled by her request and wondered what it could be about.

"Eliza dear," she said when everyone had left the room and I was standing by her desk, "I have a little something for you and your friend, Florence."

With a little tug and a jerk, she opened one of the small drawers in her old wooden desk and took out two small drawstring pouches made from soft white material.

"These are protection bags," she stated seriously. "They contain some herbs and crystals and things." Then, seeing my confused expression, she added, "To keep you girls safe."

"Um, thank you Miss Angelica," I said, feeling like I was missing some vital information. "But if you don't mind me asking, what exactly do we need to be kept safe from?"

Miss Angelica glanced around nervously, even though we were the only ones in the room.

"The Shadows," she whispered, leaning closer to me as she did so.

I frowned, not sure what she was on about. The whole conversation seemed strange and I'm ashamed to say that for a few moments I even had doubts about Miss Angelica's sanity. Then she reached into the drawer again and handed me a rolled up scroll.

"Please," she implored, "I'd like you and your friend to read this. There are many wonderful things in the world of magic. But there's evil as well. So you need to know what to look out for."

Feeling creeped out and eager to leave, I thanked Miss Angelica, stuffed the scroll in my bag and dashed off to my Friday afternoon detention. I didn't see Flo until supper that evening. I had decided not to show the scroll to Hannah and Seren, preferring to keep it a secret between Flo and me. So during supper I handed her a little note which read: 'Need to talk to you. I'll come up to your room at 7.30 pm.'

CHAPTER 11

SHADOWS AND SPELLS

Flo's roommate was a girl named Harriet. She was usually studying, and when she wasn't studying she was busy with the debating club or the maths club or the student council. She also played various musical instruments and always wore her blonde hair tied back tightly in a French plait. She was the conventional nerd, and I doubted she'd ever done anything fun in her whole life. So when I got up to Flo's room, I wasn't surprised to find that Harriet was away for the weekend, playing her flute at some concert.

"Well?" asked Flo as I sat down on her bed. "What do you need to talk to me about?"

"This," I said as I took the scroll out of my bag. "Oh and these," I added, rummaging around for the little white pouches.

Flo looked puzzled. "Ok, explain," she said.

I proceeded to tell her everything that had happened with Miss Angelica after Herbology class. She was intrigued and sat down beside me as I carefully undid the thin black cord which was fastened around the scroll. The parchment had a curious feel to it: heavier than normal paper and quite rough, as if it had been made by hand using an old, unsophisticated technique. It was discoloured from age, and covered in elegant cursive handwriting which had obviously been carried out with a traditional fountain pen and ink. This is what is said:

'Warnings and Cautions for the New Witch

The Shadows are out there. They exist, in the invisible world that parallels our own. Unlike creatures from our world, they lack physical form, and feed off energy. They range in size and power. Most are content to feed on the random energy that leaks from humans and other creatures in our world. Others, however, are more sinister. These, the ones you have to worry about, are called the Shadows.

Types of Shadows

1. The first variety are the little ones that feed off energy from negative emotions. If you are not magically protected, they will latch onto your energy field and feed on it. They are usually not too troublesome, unless you attract a considerable number of them, in which case they can weaken you severely.

2. Next comes the more dangerous variety. They are attracted both by negative emotions and the energy of magical workings. They are stronger, and can push through weak or faulty defences to get to you. And once they have their 'teeth' in you, they are dreadfully difficult to get rid of.

3.   Last is the intelligent variety. They feed off human life energy. They are relatively rare, but they exist. They are very strong. The more intelligent ones are capable of talking you into dropping your defences, in order for them to be able to link their energy field to yours. They may go as far as to promise you power beyond your wildest dreams if you open yourself to them. They are also capable of entering our world, if someone is helpful enough to open a doorway for them. And once here, they will try to get past all your defences. They can then enter your body and feed at will, even asserting a degree of control over you.

Please Stay Safe'

When we'd both finished reading, I rolled up the scroll and looked at Flo, who seemed unsettled.

"I'm sleeping with the light on from now on," she said with a nervous laugh. I thought she was joking, but I couldn't be sure.

When Flo and I walked into the attic on Saturday night, Hannah and Seren were already there, busy setting up an altar in the middle of the room. On it was a pentagram, two black candles, a small bell, a bowl of salt and one of water, the miniature sword and a chalice. They greeted us and told us to put on our robes. Seren then began to lay a red cord around the altar, forming a circle. But before closing the circle completely, she asked us all to step inside. While Hannah lit the candles, Seren spoke.

"Tonight I will cast a sacred circle," she said solemnly. "In a circle, the rules and conditions are different to those of the everyday world. A circle is a doorway to another world. Any magical energy raised will be contained in the circle until it has been used up."

Seren then closed the circle and walked around it, her sword held high in her hand. As she walked, she said, "With this sacred blade, I cast the circle of my craft. May it be a doorway to a place beyond time and space. So mote it be."

It was a warm evening and the attic felt stuffy. I glanced at the little window, tightly shut, and longed for some fresh air. Seren went to stand in front of the altar, picked up the bell and said, "In the names of the God and Goddess, I cast this, my working circle." Then she rang the bell. After this, she took the bowl of water and walked around again, this time sprinkling the water along the line of the circle. As she did this, she said, "I consecrate this sacred circle by the powers of Earth, Air, Fire and Water. She then poured some water into the chalice and sipped it, afterwards placing it on top of the pentagram. At last the casting of the circle was complete.

Seren then asked Hannah to pass her the cauldron. I hadn't noticed it before because it had been on the floor behind the altar. Seren cleared a space in the middle of the altar and placed the small black pot there.

"Tonight," she said authoritatively, "we will cast a revenge spell on five girls. I have their names written down." She gestured to some pieces of paper that were lying in the cauldron. "Now let's join hands."

Alright! I thought excitedly. *Now this is getting interesting!*

We all joined hands and Seren told us to close our eyes, clear our minds and visualise Meredith, Layla, Beatrice, Cassie and Amanda in our minds. Then she said:

Powers east, west, north and south,

Bewitch our foes who us insult;

Revenge be bitter, cruel and harsh,

I now command a swift result.

So mote it be.

Hannah used one of the black candles to set fire to the five small pieces of paper and we stood and watched them burn. Then Seren picked up her sword and said, "Guardians and spirits, my ritual is now complete. I bid you hail and farewell." Then she blew out the candles and bowed her head, saying, "I declare this sacred circle closed. So mote it be." Hannah then rang the bell and we all stepped out of the circle. It was very late and I suddenly felt incredibly tired.

***

Sunday was a muggy, clammy day. It had rained during the night and the heat had set in by mid-morning. After lunch, Flo asked if I felt like joining her for a walk. She didn't look herself, the dark bags under her eyes suggesting she hadn't had much sleep the previous night. I said I'd love a walk, and half an hour later we were ambling through the grounds in the direction of the woods. Butterflies flitted here and there amongst the flowers and bees buzzed around our heads. I was happy to observe that summer had arrived at last. Flo was very quiet and didn't say a word until we were in the woods. Then as soon as she spotted the old mossy tree stump, she flopped down dejectedly and put her head in her hands. Concerned, I knelt down in front of her.

"Flo," I said, "tell me what's wrong."

Her slumped shoulders shook and she looked very small and vulnerable. "It's everything," she sobbed, taking a great gulp of air and wiping her eyes with her sleeve. "I mean all this magic stuff and those shadows and casting spells on people. I'm scared."

"Oh Flo!" I said, enveloping her in a big hug. "It's just a bit of fun, really. Nothing bad is going to happen."

"But how do you know that?" asked Flo anxiously. "Last night kind of freaked me out. Lizzy, we cast a spell to harm people. Remember that book Miss Angelica lent us? It said stuff about not doing any harm. And there was something about karma and the consequences of our actions."

Somewhere deep down I knew Flo was probably right. But I desperately wanted to get back at the Toffees. They deserved to be put in their place once and for all.

"Look Flo," I said soothingly, "it's just a game. Nothing bad has happened so far. And you have to admit we are having fun!"

"I don't know," said Flo doubtfully. "Is it just a game? I can't shake the feeling that we don't really know what we're getting ourselves into."

"Okay," I said after a pause. "Let's make a deal. How about if we continue being part of the coven as long as nothing really bad happens? But if things get out of hand and either one of us wants out, then we're free to leave."

After a few minutes of deep thought, Flo seemed satisfied - at least for the time being. She got up and gave me a hug, saying she was exhausted and wanted to go back to her room for a nap. So we made our way back through the forest and out into the warm afternoon sunshine.

When we got to the courtyard in front of the main school building, there seemed to be quite a commotion, so we stopped to see what was going on. A large crowd had gathered, and Mrs Tupperley and another house mistress, Miss Kelly, were busy telling the girls to be on their way and that they would deal with it. As some of the girls stepped aside, we saw Meredith sitting on a bench clutching her left hand and crying almost hysterically. She seemed to be in an enormous amount of pain. Flo looked at me and I knew exactly what she was thinking.

"What happened?" I asked one of the girls who was leaving the scene.

"She got bitten by something on her hand," said the girl. "Down at the stables. Miss Kelly said it was probably a spider."

Meredith was rushed to A&E and everyone was talking about it. She was back by supper time, but was served her food in the infirmary. The story was that she'd been bitten by a False Widow Spider and was now on strong painkillers and had to rest until she felt better. Flo, of course, was terrified that our spell could have had something to do with it.

"Oh come on Flo," I said the next day at school. "Those stables are probably full of spiders. Anyone could get bitten by one. I'm sure it had nothing to do with magic."

"Well I suppose that's a rational explanation," she said eventually.

The rest of the week went by with the usual routine until Thursday evening after supper. Seren and I were sitting talking in our room when we heard screaming and shouting coming from down the hall. We immediately ran to see what was going on and it wasn't long before we realised the commotion was coming from Layla's new room. When I managed to steal a glance through the doorway, which was already crowded with people, I saw Layla standing in the middle of the room, drenched from head to foot. A large puddle of water was growing steadily around her as water trickled down from her clothes and hair. Then I noticed that the ceiling above her bed and desk had fallen in, obviously bringing a deluge of water with it. The bed was completely soaked, as was the desk on which her top-of-the-range laptop computer lay open.

"Somebody do something!" Layla screeched angrily, looking like she'd just been dragged out of a river. "Don't just stand there like a bunch of gaping fools! I need help!"

The whole scene was actually hilarious, and Seren gave me a high-five as we walked cheerfully back to our room.

"Two down, three to go!" she said triumphantly.

I tossed and turned in bed that night, wondering whether there could really be a connection between the spell and the recent mishaps. I also thought Flo would probably need placating again after this latest incident.   As long as nothing worse happens everything will be alright, I told myself, falling into fitful sleep at last.

By Monday morning, everyone had heard about Layla's soaking. Most people found it funny, and I think because of this, Flo wasn't as troubled as I had expected her to be. It was discovered that a burst pipe above Layla's room had caused the ceiling to cave in, and Flo admitted that it could have happened to anyone. I didn't tell her of my surprise when I'd noticed Layla's roommate's side of the room was bone dry and completely unaffected.

Then on Wednesday during our English lesson, Cassie was caught writing a love letter to a boy when we were supposed to be working on a piece of creative writing. Mrs Stokes was really angry and told Cassie to come and see her straight after school, as she had some work for her to do. Cassie just rolled her eyes as Mrs Stokes turned her back, and I didn't think any more about it. Then that evening at supper, I noticed there was a lot of whispering and giggling going on. When Flo took her seat next to me, she said, "You'll never guess what happened!"

"What?" I asked expectantly. But just then Cassie walked into the dining hall and everyone fell silent. Her hair, which had been so long and beautiful, was now sitting just under her ears in a very unusual (or rather ugly) style. I couldn't imagine what had possessed her to have it cut like that.

"It was an accident," whispered Flo, noting my surprise. "Mrs Stokes had her shredding paper this afternoon as punishment, and her hair got caught in the shredder. They say she's lucky it wasn't any worse."

"Nice one, don't you think?" said Seren with a smirk. "Not so gorgeous now, is she?"

I think Flo was in denial, because she said nothing more about the recent incidents. Seren was convinced they were due to the spell, and we often sat up at night, eagerly trying to guess what might happen to the other two Toffees, Beatrice and Amanda. Seren said the spell was probably powerful enough for one bad thing to happen to each of the girls.

Everything was quiet again until the following Tuesday evening. Flo happened to be in the bathroom in Churchill House when Beatrice came in looking very agitated. Her face was apparently very red and blotchy, and Flo said she was making things worse by frantically scratching her cheeks 'til they bled. Then just as Flo asked if she was okay, Beatrice began to wheeze alarmingly, so Flo ran to called Miss Kelly. As it turned out, Beatrice was having an allergic reaction to a new moisturising cream. Miss Kelly had to give her an injection, and she spent the night in the infirmary. I noticed Flo seemed slightly uneasy as she related the event. *Oh no,* I thought, *she's having her doubts again.*

CHAPTER 12

ARE THERE ANY SPIRITS PRESENT?

After this incident, everything seemed to go back to normal. Life went on, and we were looking forward to spending another pleasant Saturday in the local town. The weather was gloriously sunny and warm, and there was an arts and crafts market as well as a cricket match scheduled, so there was more to see and do than usual. Seren had brought a big backpack with her and as we walked across the bridge into town, Hannah asked what was in it.

"Nothing," Seren replied. "It's empty."

"Oh good," I said, grinning. "Then we can all stuff our hats and ties in it and you can carry them around for us all day!"

Seren laughed and told us there was no chance of that happening. Then she said she was going to meet Dylan and that she'd find us somewhere later.

"I hate the way she always ditches us," Hannah said grumpily as soon as Seren was out of earshot.

"I think her and Dylan are really into each other," I said.

"Yeah well I think Dylan's a bad influence on her," scoffed Hannah.

I think we all suspected that was true. Dylan seemed very introverted, never made eye contact, and didn't speak to any of us except Seren. I thought he looked troubled and withdrawn - the classic 'bad boy.' But we left it at that and talked about our plans for the day. We decided on a walk around the arts and crafts market before going over to the sports field to watch the cricket match. Of course we had no interest in cricket; it was just nice to get the chance to ogle some boys for a change.

The day passed blissfully as we lazed around on the grass in the warm sunshine, chatting and laughing while eating a picnic lunch in view of the match. We were terribly disappointed when we realised it was time to start our walk back to school. But we still hadn't seen Seren anywhere, and we didn't really want to leave her behind, so we took a quick walk around town to see if we could find her. As we rounded a corner past the old, ivy-covered stone church, we spotted her and Dylan coming out of the churchyard. Hannah waved to get Seren's attention, and she hurried over to join us. Dylan didn't follow; he just stayed where he was in the graveyard, like some unfathomable apparition.

It was obvious that Seren had something quite big and heavy in her backpack. She was a small girl, and the weight of the bag was causing her to lean forward in order to keep her balance. Hannah, who still looked annoyed with her, asked what was in it. I think she was a bit jealous that Seren had a boyfriend and she didn't.

"I'll enlighten you in due course," said Seren cryptically, which seemed to enrage Hannah even more.

"Come on, tell us!" she demanded. "We're your friends!"

Seren walked on in silence, seemingly deep in thought. Eventually she said, "I won't tell you what it is – I'll show you what it is. But not until next Saturday night in the attic."

***

It was summertime, the weather was glorious, and school sport was in full swing. Hannah was on the Thatcher lacrosse team, and the girls practiced almost every day. They were very good - even scarily aggressive at times. Amanda was captain and she clearly expected her team to win at all costs. Seren, Flo and I would often go and watch the girls practice. Thatcher was definitely the best team, exciting to watch and at that stage, still unbeaten.

On the Wednesday afternoon following our Saturday in town, Seren, Flo and I strolled down to the lacrosse field after school. It was a sweltering day and most of us were dressed in our sports kit because it was cooler and so much more comfortable than school uniform. It consisted of a white golf shirt with the school logo in the top right hand corner, a pair of purple and blue checked culottes, long sky blue socks and white trainers.

That day we sat down gratefully in the cool shade of the stands to watch the game in progress. It was only a practice match, but it was still exciting. Thatcher was playing Atlee and no one had scored yet. I could see the girls were taking strain in the heat and pouring with sweat. But they all seemed tenacious, and carried on regardless.

And then suddenly it happened. Amanda had just managed to get the ball away from Willow when she started to run and turn at the same time. Her left foot slid out from under her, and she seemed to try to regain her balance, but her ankle was already bent and she fell really hard. Miss Jackson, the coach, blew the whistle to stop the game. Amanda tried to get up, but quickly sat down again, her face contorted in agony. Miss Jackson and Meredith helped her up and she managed to hop as far as the stands. Then she just collapsed, holding her ankle and crying from the pain. A few minutes later Mrs Garnett arrived in her car. Amanda was helped in and they sped off, presumably to the Accident and Emergency department at the local hospital.

When all the drama was over and we were the only ones left in the stands, Seren turned to us and said, "Yes! That's all five taken care of then. Well done, my fellow witches!"

***

Meredith had by now fully recovered from her spider bite, and Layla was bragging to everyone about the new MacBook Pro her dad had bought her to replace the laptop which had been ruined in the flood. Beatrice was fine after her allergic reaction, but said she had to be careful about what products she used in future. Cassie still fretted constantly about her hair, even though everyone was growing tired of her constant moaning and told her it would grow again. As for Amanda - she had suffered a badly sprained ankle and was now hobbling around on crutches. Meredith actually seemed pleased about Amanda's bad luck, because it meant she could take over as captain of Thatcher's lacrosse team!

I met up with Flo on Friday afternoon after detention. We had decided to go for a nice relaxing swim in the new indoor pool. The weather had been so hot lately and we thought a swim would be cool and refreshing. The pool was in a brand new gymnasium, separate from the rest of the school, but built in the same style so that it fitted in with the appearance of the property. There were squash courts, a well-equipped gym area with circuit training, and the swimming pool. The wall on the far side of the pool was made of one-way glass panels, so you could look out over the grounds while you were swimming, but no one could see in. It was all very tastefully designed and made me feel like I'd just entered one of those posh and very expensive health and fitness clubs.

Flo and I were surprisingly the only ones in the pool that afternoon. We swam a few lengths in a rather lazy fashion, then just chilled out in the water, chatting.

"I wonder what Seren's going to show us tomorrow night," I said.

A brief shadow of unease pass over Flo's face before she said, "I don't have a clue what it is, but I'll bet it's got something to do with that awful boyfriend of hers."

"I don't know about awful," I said distractedly. "Maybe good-looking and mysterious..."

"Lizzy, he's a total weirdo!" said Flo in exasperation. "He doesn't talk, he dresses like a cross between a rocker and a tramp, and I wouldn't be surprised if he's on drugs."

"Oh Flo!" I said, laughing. "I don't think he's that bad! But I'm just so curious about whatever Seren's going to show us tomorrow. Do you know that she's hidden that backpack? I tried looking for it when she was out - you know, to sneak a little peek - but it was absolutely nowhere."

"She's probably hidden it up in the attic," said Flo matter-of-factly.

"Of course!" I exclaimed in amazement. "You genius! Why didn't I think of that?"

"Let's just be patient and wait for tomorrow night," said Flo. "The last thing we need is to get caught sneaking up to the attic in broad daylight."

On Saturday afternoon, Hannah, Seren, Flo and I watched a lacrosse game down on the main field. It was our first school team playing another school called St Helen's. It was a really exciting game and we all enjoyed cheering for our school, which eventually won the game in great style. The heat was becoming more and more intense, though, and we were thankful for the shade of the stands. I noticed the grass was looking brown and dry and all the plants were wilting. But by evening, storm clouds were building up on the horizon and everyone was hoping for a good shower of rain.

***

My phone vibrated at a quarter to twelve that night, waking me in time for our midnight rendezvous. I was already dressed and so was Seren, so we just slipped on our shoes and made our way silently over to the main school building. Hannah and Flo were already waiting for us in the foyer, and the four of us wasted no time in climbing up the many dark, narrow staircases which led us to top floor.

The attic was stiflingly hot and the only window was the poky little one high up in one of the walls. Hannah, being the tallest, managed to reach it by standing on one of the wooden chairs. Then, with some difficulty, she eventually succeeded in lifting the rusty old latch and pushing open the window, letting in a welcome gust of cooler air.

"Right girls," said Seren, turning to face us. "We won't be using the altar tonight, so we don't have to worry about setting it up."

She asked Hannah to light some candles and turn off the overhead light. Once that had been done, she told us to sit on the rug, cross-legged in a circle, with our knees touching. Seren then went over to the old cupboard and returned with a heavy wooden board. She set it down carefully on the floor in the middle of our circle before taking her place between Hannah and me. Intrigued, I studied the unfamiliar item and thought it must be some kind of Victorian board game, used for entertainment in the days when there was no radio or television. On the top two corners were the words 'YES' and 'NO'. Then there were the letters A to Z, and underneath those, the numbers zero to nine. At the bottom of the board was the word 'GOODBYE', and there was a sun and moon set into the wood. To be honest, I didn't think it looked terribly exciting, so I was puzzled when Flo turned pale and began to get upset.

"I don't, I mean I…" she began fretfully, uncrossing her legs and standing up.

"Flo, it's only a spirit board; it's not going to jump up and bite you!" said Seren, trying to ease Flo's obvious distress.

"It's a Ouija board!" said Flo anxiously. "I've read about them! They can be really dangerous! What if a bad spirit comes through?"

"Okay just calm down," said Seren soothingly. "I know what can happen with these things. Dylan and I have played around with this one lots of times. But I always make sure I do a protection ritual first.

Nothing can harm you if you're properly protected. So just give it a chance, okay?"

Hannah and I also encouraged Flo, and at last she sat down. Seren then proceeded to place a piece of heart-shaped wood on the board. She explained that it was called a planchette or a pointer, and that when you put your fingers on it, it should move around the board once contact has been made with an entity from the other side. I thought it sounded wildly exciting, but I was also more than a bit sceptical, and doubted that anything would actually happen.

After doing a short protection ritual, Seren said it was time to start the séance. As she showed us how to place our index and middle fingers lightly on the pointer, thunder rumbled in the distance and I felt a shiver run down my spine.

"Are there any spirits present who would like to come forward and communicate with us?" asked Seren. There wasn't a sound except for the thunder which rumbled again in the distance. Seren patiently repeated her question while we waited expectantly for something to happen.

"When you are ready please move the pointer to 'YES' or move it in circles," she said.

Then all of a sudden, with no warning, the pointer began to move erratically, shuffling all over the board before coming to rest on the word 'YES.' I wondered briefly if Seren could have been messing around and moving the pointer herself, when the room abruptly turned cold and the atmosphere became eerie. My heartbeat quickened as Seren cleared her throat and spoke again.

"Did you live on earth at any time?" she asked.

The pointer stayed where it was.

"I'll take that as a 'yes'," said Seren, before asking, "When did you leave your physical body?"

The pointer moved to the numbers 1-8-6-7.

"Thank you. Did you ever live in this building?"

There was a big crack of thunder and I felt Flo jump. The pointer quickly moved to the word 'YES'.

"What did you do for a living?"

The word 'MAID' was spelled out.

"Thank you," said Seren. "Now please tell us your name."

The spirit seemed to hesitate, because nothing happened for a few minutes. Then there was a hair-raising crash just behind Seren and Hannah as a large glass vase fell from the top of the old wooden cupboard. We all jumped in fright.

"Please only use the board to communicate!" Seren commanded, as the atmosphere began to feel more sinister.

"What is your name?" she asked again. This time the pointer moved to the letter 'M.' We waited for it to move again, but nothing happened. Then a powerful draught suddenly blew through the open window, causing the candles to flicker wildly and I started to feel really scared.

"Okay," said Seren calmly. "Please tell us why you came to communicate with us tonight."

There was a flash of lightning and another crack of thunder. As the lightning lit up Flo's face, I could see that she was absolutely terrified.

Then the pointer began to dart all over the board, and we became aware of a strange knocking noise coming from one of the walls. Seren looked worried for a few seconds, then quickly moved the pointer to the word 'GOODBYE.'

"Goodbye," she said authoritatively. "It's time to leave now."

I could feel my heart hammering away in my chest, as Hannah hurried to turn on the overhead light. She then ran over to close the window, as it had started to rain heavily. We all sat and looked at each other, dazed by what had happened and not quite knowing what to say. It was Seren who broke the silence at last.

"Well that didn't go quite as expected," she said with a shrug.

"Do you think we really contacted a spirit from the other side?" I asked incredulously.

"Oh we made contact, all right," said Seren with mock amusement. "But with who or what I couldn't say. You never really know what's going to happen, and the outcome of these things is often unpredictable. But that's what makes it interesting. Now I need a cigarette."

CHAPTER 13

PARANORMAL ACTIVITY

We had torrential rain in the early hours of Sunday morning, which continued well into the afternoon. Flo and I had made a plan to meet in the library that day and work on our geography projects. I had just laid out my work on one of the long wooden tables when Flo walked in. And by the look on her face, I knew I had to brace myself for another one of her emotional outpourings. At first I used to feel genuinely sorry for her, but by now I was becoming tired of her slightly pathetic attitude.

Flo walked up to the table and dropped her books on the hard surface, causing a loud thud to echo through the large, high-ceilinged room. I was a bit taken aback because it wasn't like her to be so noisy in the library. Then, without a word, she simply pulled out a chair, sat down and stared into space.

She must be exhausted from last night, I thought. I was also tired, but we really needed to finish our projects as they were due in on Tuesday and we still had so much to do.

"You look exhausted," I said. "But don't worry; we'll finish quickly if we work together."

Flo continued to stare straight ahead, her eyes glazed and her expression blank.

"Come on Flo," I said, poking her in the shoulder with my finger, "let's get started. It'll be better than having to do it all tomorrow after school."

Flo's body suddenly twitched a few times and she looked around, frowning. She seemed a bit confused for a minute, almost disorientated, and then her demeanour changed abruptly as she smiled and said, "Okay. Let's get started."

We ended up working all afternoon, and by five o'clock our assignments on 'The Woodland Ecosystem' were just about finished. Flo had been her normal self after snapping out of her earlier daze, but I was surprised that she hadn't even mentioned the previous night's 'entertainment.' I would have actually liked to discuss it, and heard Flo's point of view, but on the other hand I didn't want to risk setting her off again.

***

In assembly on Monday morning, Mrs Garnett told us about a new community project that our year group would soon be participating in. It would involve going into town on Tuesday and Friday afternoons for three weeks, and doing our choice of voluntary work. We could choose between: reading to the elderly, cleaning up the streams and park areas, or helping at the local animal shelter. Mrs Garnett gave a long speech about 'giving back to our community' and told us the project would help 'build character.' Everyone sat up and took note, not because we were genuinely interested in serving our community, but because of the splendid thought of being able to escape school for six whole afternoons!

Then later that day, something extremely weird happened. It was the strangest thing I'd ever witnessed in my whole life up to that point. I'd gone up to talk to Flo in her room, but when I knocked nobody answered. I was sure Flo was in, so I opened the door and popped my head in. There was no sign of Harriet, but Flo was sitting on her bed, staring straight ahead like she'd done the other day in the library. It looked like she was in a trance, and she didn't respond when I walked in. After watching her uneasily for a couple of minutes, I went over and snapped my fingers in front of her eyes. At first she continued to stare straight through me, but then slowly she regained her focus, and eventually looked up at me with a friendly smile.

"Hi Lizzy," she said cheerfully.

"Flo, what on earth were you doing?" I asked, still puzzled by what I had witnessed.

"What do you mean?" asked Flo, looking confused. "I wasn't doing anything. I mean other than sitting here waiting for you."

"You looked really far away, that's all. Like you were very deep in thought. It seemed as if you weren't even aware that I came into your room."

Flo said nothing, but gave me such a doubtful look that I wondered if I could have somehow imagined the whole bizarre episode. But I just shrugged and changed the subject, and we sat and talked about what we'd chosen to do for our community projects. Flo was telling me that she wasn't sure whether to read to the elderly or clean up the parks and streams. She said she'd thought about helping at the animal shelter, but couldn't face the task of cleaning litter trays. I was just saying how I'd prefer to be outdoors on nice warm summery days, when I heard a scratching noise coming from under Flo's bed.

"Did you hear that?" I asked. "Flo I think you may have a mouse in here!"

"Oh that." said Flo, looking weary. "I've been hearing it for a while now, but there's no sign of a mouse or anything else. Miss Kelly even put a trap down last week and we checked it every day but it was always empty. So now I just try my best to ignore it."

No wonder she has dark bags under her eyes, I thought. *That scratching noise must be keeping her awake all night.*

We had just gone back to talking about how pleased we were to be getting a few ours out of school for the next few weeks, when something very curious happened. Out of the corner of my eye, I was certain I had seen Flo's desk chair move. But it was far enough away that neither of us could have bumped it. I stopped talking and stared at the chair.

"Flo," I said, perplexed, "maybe I'm going mad, but I'm sure I just saw your desk chair move."

To my surprise, Flo looked delighted when I said that.

"You saw it too!" she said excitedly. "I can't tell you how relieved I am! I was convinced I was going crazy!"

I stared at her in disbelief. "So it's happened before? Flo, how long has this been going on?"

"Well," she said uncertainly, "I suppose about a fortnight now. And it's not only the chair. Other things seem to move on their own too.

Just yesterday I was sitting right here when my school hat lifted off that hook and seemed to hover in mid-air for a few seconds before landing on the floor."

I got up and went to inspect the hat which was hanging benignly on its hook. I tried bumping it and flicking it off, but the hook was at such an acute angle that I actually had to lift the hat up and over it, in order to get it off. Something very strange was going on, and I had no idea what it was.

***

Flo, Seren, Hannah and I had all decided to do the 'environment project,' which involved checking the local streams and parkland for rubbish such as food and drink cans, glass bottles, food wrappers, plastic bags and other items that could be hazardous to birds and animals. We were to sort the various items of litter into separate sacks according to the type of material they were made from, so they could be recycled.

Our first Tuesday afternoon in town saw us enjoying glorious summer weather. We made our way down the hill after lunch without any teachers, as Mrs Garnett had said she was sure we were mature enough to be trusted to do the work unsupervised. I was just wondering about the wisdom of that decision, when I spotted Dylan leaning against the bridge into town, smoking a cigarette. I wondered why he never seemed to be at work.

Then suddenly Seren turned to us and said, "Look guys, I'm really sorry but I'm going to have to ditch you today. I'll make up for it on Friday. Promise."

And with that she jogged over to Dylan, who embraced her passionately. We continued to stare in disbelief as the two off them strolled off hand in hand. Hannah looked shocked.

"I can't believe her!" she said in disgust.

I just shrugged and shook my head. Flo looked annoyed but kept her thoughts to herself.

"Let's just go and get started," she said.

We ended up having a really good time that afternoon. It was hot enough for water fights, and we knew our clothes would probably be dry by the time we'd walked back to school. We did manage to get some work done though, cleaning up quite a long stretch of stream that ran through the bottom of town and past the sports field. With an hour to go before we had to return to school, the three of us had filled two sacks with mainly drinks cans and glass bottles, along with one that was full of plastic bags and other rubbish for landfill. We'd been told to leave the filled sacks in an empty shed next to the churchyard before we left, so we made our way up there, soggy and sweaty but in good spirits.

After dumping the sacks in the shed, Flo suggested we have a rest in the shade before beginning our walk back to school. So we found a nice spot under some beech trees in the churchyard where the grass had recently been cut. It felt good to sit down and do nothing for a few minutes. But as I relaxed back against a tree trunk and took a long, much needed drink from my water bottle, my attention was drawn to a nearby headstone. Feeling curious, I inched closer so I could read the faded inscription on the small rough stone. It said:

In Memory of

Miriam Marston

Died 18 June 1867

Aged 19 years

RIP

"What does it say?" asked Hannah, who was watching me inquisitively.

"Some poor girl named Miriam Marston died in the nineteenth century. She was only nineteen," I said.

"Shame, so young," said Hannah sadly. "I wonder how she died."

"Probably cholera or plague or smallpox or something like that. I think all those awful diseases were pretty common in those days," I said, yawning and starting to feel sleepy.

I had just closed my eyes when I heard Hannah's concerned voice.

"Flo?" she said. "Flo, are you alright?"

I opened my eyes, momentarily dazzled by then bright sun, and noticed that Flo appeared to be in a trance again.

"Oh no, not again!" I said.

"Does she do this often then?" asked Hannah, her brow furrowed with concern.

"It's only started recently," I said. "It's like she's in a trance or something. She usually snaps out of it in a couple of minutes though."

"She looks kind of creepy like that," said Hannah uneasily.

We continued to observe Flo, who just gazed into the distance with a vacant expression. She didn't respond when we called her name, and I thought it seemed as though she was there in body only - her mind having left and gone off somewhere else entirely. Then suddenly there was a rustling in the tree above her and Hannah and I both jumped in fright. It was only a crow, but it cawed so loudly that it seemed to rouse Flo from her trance. She blinked a few times, picked up her water bottle as if nothing had happened, and announced that it must be time to go back to school.

Seren caught up with us on our way out of town, apologising again for having deserted us. She seemed in very high spirits, and said she had something really exciting planned for us.

"I hope it doesn't involve Dylan," said Hannah sullenly.

Seren stopped in her tracks. "What have you got against Dylan?" she asked hotly. "What's he ever done to you?"

Hannah rolled her eyes and stomped off.

"Anyway," Seren continued, ignoring Hannah and turning to Flo and me, "this Friday there'll be a full moon, so I'm organising a séance in the churchyard!"

"What, in broad daylight?" I asked in surprise.

"No, silly!" said Seren, grinning impishly. "We'll sneak out of school at night."

Feeling a bit alarmed, I looked over at Flo. Neither of us had ever sneaked off the school property before, and I knew if we were caught it would mean we'd be permanently excluded from school. And that wasn't really a chance I wanted to take.

"That sounds like a thoroughly cool idea," said Flo unexpectedly, catching me off-guard. I thought my ears must be deceiving me.

"Whoa!" I said, holding up both hands. "Let's just think about this for a minute. Don't you think it's a bit risky? I mean what if we get caught?"

Seren and Flo exchanged amused looks before Seren turned to me and said, "Well suit yourself, Miss Goodie-Two-Shoes. No one's forcing you to come."

***

Friday dawned grey and overcast. It was one of those really muggy days, and I felt sticky and irritable. I still hadn't made up my mind about the séance. I knew it would be risky, but I didn't want to be the odd one out. Flo, Seren and Hannah were my only friends at Hilltop Hall and I couldn't afford to lose them. I mulled over the problem all day, which made it impossible to concentrate on my lessons.

After lunch we set off for another afternoon of 'character-building' (if only Mrs Garnett knew!) community work. Seren brought along her big backpack, which she said was full of things for the séance. She planned on hiding it in a dense thicket somewhere along the perimeter of the churchyard. As we walked, Hannah, Seren and Flo talked excitedly about the evening ahead, while I trudged along next to them, not sure how to feel about it.

Seren joined in with the work that day, stopping every now and then for a 'smoke break.' I wondered why she smoked when everyone knew it caused cancer, but I never said anything about it. I think the afternoon's work helped clear my head, because I soon started feeling a lot more optimistic. My friends' enthusiasm must have had an effect on me, and by the time we began our walk back to school, I was even feeling a twinge of excitement about the night ahead.

***.

Dressed all in black so we'd be more difficult to spot, we snuck out just after eleven that night. We didn't use the main gate, choosing instead to go around the back of the school and through the woods. It was a much longer route, but safer for us because we thought it unlikely we'd be noticed that way. The overcast sky made the night darker than it should have been in June, and the air was still and clammy. We made our way quickly and quietly, staying close together, with Seren leading the way. Shadows seemed to lurk behind every tree in the woods, tormenting us as we made our way cautiously over serpent-like, gnarled roots. The worry in my mind about being caught was soon suppressed by a peculiar thrill of fear and excitement. At last we emerged from the dark, eerie woods, finding ourselves on the winding path which led the way to Miss Angelica's little cottage. All was in total darkness as we crept soundlessly past before continuing hurriedly on our way.

A narrow, meandering footpath led us through fields towards the town. Some sheep bleated and scattered frantically as our unexpected appearance disturbed them from their peaceful slumber. As we continued down the hill, I could see lights glowing in the distance. I'd never been to town this way, and was surprised to find that the route eventually ended in a copse of trees at the back of the churchyard. Seren and Hannah seemed to know exactly where they were going, so

I presumed they'd been that way before. My eyes were now quite accustomed to the dark, and it wasn't long before I could make out the ancient gravestones through gaps in the dense trees. In the dim light, it was easy to imagine them as figures of the living dead - silently rising up out of the ground, faceless and lurching drunkenly in all directions. Then suddenly I heard a deep cough, which brought me back to reality with a start.

Who on earth could be lurking in the churchyard at this time of night? I thought uneasily, before realising we were doing just that. Then, as we came to the clearing under the trees where we'd been on Tuesday afternoon, I spotted a tall dark figure and nearly jumped out of my skin.

"Greetings, Alim, oh wise and learned one," said Seren, as she took a little bow.

On closer inspection, I recognised the figure as Dylan.

Why on earth is she calling him Alim? I wondered, bemused. *Must be some kind of loony-tune game.*

Then Dylan said, "Greetings Seren, oh enchanted star."

Okay, I thought, noticing the puzzled expressions on Hannah and Flo's faces. *I guess we'll just have to play along.*

Seren handed out the robes and instructed us to put them on. I noticed Dylan was already wearing a robe, but it was different to ours' - black with a red lining and more like a cloak. Seren then did a short protection ritual while Dylan lit some candles. A blanket had been laid out on the ground and in the middle was the Ouija board. On Seren's command, we all sat down around it, and as we did so, the already muggy air thickened noticeably. Everything was suddenly very quiet and still and I shivered in spite of the warm evening. Then we all placed our fingers lightly on the pointer as the séance began.

"Is there anyone here who would like to communicate with us tonight?" asked Seren.

Some leaves rustled sinisterly in the trees around us, despite the absence of a breeze.

"Please use the board to communicate. I ask again if there are any spirits present who would like to communicate with us," said Seren firmly.

The pointer seemed to vibrate slightly before moving directly to the word 'YES.'

"Can you tell us your name?"

The pointer slowly spelled out the phrase 'I AM HERE', as the atmosphere underwent another subtle change.

"Please could you spell out your name," Seren said patiently.

This time the pointer moved to the letters M-I-R and then stopped.

"Mir?" asked Seren. "That doesn't sound like a real name. Is that your name?"

The pointer then moved slowly to the letters I-A-M.

"I am…" said Seren doubtfully, then, "Miriam! Yes, that's a good name, thank you!"

Then suddenly it hit me. *Miriam!* That was the name of the girl who was buried just a few feet from us! *Could it be?* I wondered, nudging Hannah. She turned and looked at me with wide eyes as Seren continued to ask the spirit questions.

"How old were you when you died?"

The pointer moved to the numbers 1-9, and I drew in a deep breath of air.

"Thank you," said Seren. "Now could you please tell us how you died?"

All of a sudden the pointer began to move haphazardly, darting around the board before stopping on the word 'YES.'

"Please tell us how you died," Seren said again.

An owl hooted and leaves rustled mysteriously as we waited for a response, our eyes glued to the board. Then suddenly my attention was diverted as I became aware of Flo, who had begun to jerk and twitch disturbingly beside me. For a moment it looked like she was having a fit, but then she began to speak.

"I...I was..." she began. Everyone turned to look at her, stunned. The words were definitely coming out of Flo's mouth, but it wasn't her voice. It sounded like a woman with a Welsh accent.

"I was pushed," she said at last, staring straight ahead with glazed eyes.

"Where were you pushed Miriam?" Seren asked steadily, looking intently at Flo.

"Down the stairs," said Flo quietly. "Down, down, down." Then she covered her face with her hands and her body shook with great, heart-breaking sobs.

I hesitantly put my arm around her shoulders, but she shrugged me off forcefully. Then she stood up and, moaning and weeping, staggered towards the small headstone which bore the name 'Miriam

Marston.' We all watched in silence as she sat down on the grave, staring straight ahead. I was scared. In fact I felt a bit panicked. I wasn't sure what was happening, and the whole thing felt surreal. I wanted to help Flo, but I didn't know what to do. So I just sat there and did what everyone else was doing - I gawked helplessly at poor Flo.

I'm not sure how much time passed. Nobody said or did anything for what seemed like an eternity. Everything was still except for Flo, who sobbed and shuddered intermittently. Then, at last, even Flo was silent.

"CAW!"

"Oh my gosh, what the hell was that?" screamed Seren, sounding terrified.

"A crow!" replied Dylan. "In the middle of the night! How about that!"

Hannah and I were clutching each other, our hearts pounding. I glanced over at Flo, who was looking at us with a confused expression on her face.

"What just happened?" she asked, frowning.

"You just freaked us all out," said Seren, walking over to where Flo was sitting. "Hey, Dyl! Bring your lighter over here; I want to have a look at something."

Dylan hurried over and Seren held the lighter up to the headstone.

"You guys have got to come and see this."

"We know what it says," said Hannah. "We saw it on Tuesday."

As we walked back up the long winding path and through the dark, sinister woods, I couldn't shake the feeling that I was being watched. I was sure someone –or something- was following me.

CHAPTER 14

IT'S TIME TO FINISH THIS

Everything changed after that night in the churchyard. At first, the magic and revenge and everything that came with it had seemed like a bit of harmless fun and amusement, but now it was beginning to feel different. It seemed to be consuming our lives, like some kind of weird addiction. We were totally obsessed and craved the thrill we got from being able to communicate with spirits through the board. And we'd virtually forgotten about the Toffees, who were so immersed in their busy schedule of summer horse shows that they'd ceased to pay us any attention.

Also, strange things had started happening to us. We felt like we were never alone, even when we were. The Saturday after the séance, when Seren and I were getting ready for bed, our door opened and slammed shut. The bedroom windows were closed, and when we opened the door and checked the corridor, there was nobody there.

What was really worrying, though, were the things that were happening to Flo. On the Monday afternoon after the séance, I went to see her in her room. When I got there, she was cleaning up some sort of mess on the floor.

"Hi Flo!" I said cheerfully. "What you up to?"

"Just cleaning up this mess," she said. "Remember those little white bags Miss Angelica gave us? With the herbs and crystals and stuff in? Well when I got up here a few minutes ago, I found mine lying open, with the contents spilled all over the floor."

"Your protection bag," I stated, feeling a twinge of alarm.

"Yes, that's it," said Flo. "To be honest, I'd forgotten all about it. I remember tossing it in one of my desk drawers after you gave it to me, but I've never even thought about it since."

"Flo!" I admonished. "You're supposed to keep that bag with you when we do magic and séances and stuff! It's meant to keep you safe from like, evil shadows and things, remember? I always make sure I've got mine in my pocket."

Flo looked thoughtful for a minute, then continued cleaning up the last of the scattered herbs. I thought she seemed tense and jittery. Then our attention was diverted by three loud knocks, which seemed to have come from the room next door. Seconds later, the door swung open and a girl appeared, looking annoyed.

"What's going on in here?" she demanded angrily. "I've got a pounding headache; could you please keep it down?"

"We were just talking," Flo said mildly. "We thought the noise was coming from your side."

"Of course it wasn't!" the girl spat crossly. Then she mumbled, "Something odd's going on in here," as she left.

Flo and I looked at each other. A few weeks ago we would have laughed about it, but now we just couldn't shake the feeling that something wasn't quite right.

"It's getting worse," Flo whispered after a moment.

"Maybe we should stop, you know, the magic and stuff."

Flo looked at me, her expression solemn. Then her eyes glazed over and with a Welsh accent that unnerved me to the depths of my core, she chuckled wickedly, "It's too late for that!"

***

That night I couldn't sleep. I kept seeing strange shadows moving around my bed. Glancing over at Seren, I was annoyed to see that she appeared to be sleeping soundly. I decided to pull my duvet up over my head and try to get some rest, but after about five minutes I gave up - it was just far too hot. I lay for a while and listened to the wind getting up outside, then switched on my bedside lamp and tried to read. I felt a bit more at ease with the light on, and the book was a welcome distraction. After a while I began to feel sleepy and could feel myself starting to doze off. Then the next minute there was a loud crash, and I jumped out of bed, shaking. Frantically surveying the room, I saw that Seren's coffee mug had fallen off her desk and smashed to pieces on the floor.

"What the hell was that?!" shrieked Seren, before her eyes came to rest on the pieces of broken pottery lying on the floor. "Hey!" she exclaimed, "How did that happen?"

My heart was beating almost out of my chest.

"I was just lying on my bed, reading," I said, still in shock. "I wasn't anywhere near it."

Seren swung her legs out of bed and rubbed her eyes.

"This is getting crazy," she said, shaking her head.

"I know!" I said. "Which is why I think we should just forget about the magic and the séances and just get rid of that Ouija board and..."

"No!" said Seren forcefully. "No! Miriam needs our help! We have to finish what we started!"

I stared at her in disbelief.

"Besides," she added cryptically, "I don't think Miriam's ready to let us go."

***

The following morning when we took our seats in English class, I glanced over at Hannah, who was looking pale and drawn. She had her jumper and blazer on, despite the summer warmth. Even Mrs Stokes noticed, and asked if she was feeling unwell. Hannah said she had a headache, so Mrs Stokes sent her to the school nurse.

I didn't see Hannah again that morning, but at lunch time, Seren, Flo and I decided to go and see if she was in the infirmary. We found her lying on one of the beds, resting.

"Hey Hannah," said Seren, "How's your headache?"

Hannah opened her eyes and regarded us, her expression stony.

"I don't have a headache," she said. "I'm just tired; I didn't get much sleep last night."

I felt uneasy when she said that, and knew something must have happened to keep her awake.

"What happened?" I asked, not sure if I really wanted to know.

Hannah looked upset, like she was about to cry.

"Someone - or something - kept pulling the sheet off my bed last night," she began shakily. "It was too hot for a duvet, so I just covered with a sheet. I was just drifting off to sleep when I thought I saw a shadowy figure moving around near my desk. Then all of a sudden the sheet was snatched right off me and onto the floor. Of course I screamed, which woke Lucy, so I told her I'd had a nightmare. But then it happened three more times."

I felt my gut lurch. No one said anything. We all just stared at the floor. Eventually Seren broke the silence.

"Ok," she began, "I think it's time to finish this. I suspect part of the problem is that we didn't shut the board down after the séance in the churchyard. But I think the main thing is that Miriam needs our help. Her spirit is stuck here, on the physical plane. We need to find out who pushed her down the stairs, and why. Her spirit needs to be put to rest, because if it's not, then…"

"Then we'll get no rest either," Flo finished for her.

Seren nodded. "Tomorrow night," she said. "In the attic."

***

Tuesday dawned wild and windy, and it felt like cooler weather was on the way. The morning passed quickly, and the afternoon was taken up with our 'voluntary' work in town. We were all quite subdued that day; there wasn't any of the fun messing around that we'd enjoyed the previous week. The blustery wind seemed to bring more rubbish with it, but we just got on with the task and were soon on our way back to school.

By eleven o'clock that night the wind was howling tempestuously. We made our way quickly up to the attic and lit some candles. We didn't bother with robes or a ceremony or anything like that. There was an unnerving sense of urgency as Seren set the board on the floor and did a short protection ritual. The wind seemed to wail through every tiny space, and the candles flickered continuously. It was a wild, eerie night, and the window pane shook in its frame as we all placed our fingers on the pointer.

"Tonight," Seren said loudly, having to almost shout over the sound of the wind, "we would like to communicate with the spirit of Miriam Marston. Miriam, if you are present, please give us a sign."

For a few moments nothing happened, but the temperature in the attic dropped noticeably and I shivered. Then, quite unexpectedly, the wind dropped and everything became dead quiet. You could have heard a pin drop. The candles stopped flickering and we became aware of footsteps approaching the attic. My heart raced as the door creaked slowly open and then closed again. The footsteps continued across the floor, getting closer to us until they stopped just behind Flo.

"Thank you," said Seren. "You may now communicate with us using the board."

As if in answer, the pointer moved through the numbers on the board, counting down from nine to zero. I noticed Seren looked uneasy. Hannah held a pen and note pad, ready to jot down any information we received.

"Miriam," Seren said authoritatively, "we'd like to help you but we need some more facts. So my first question is: who pushed you down the stairs?"

The pointer slowly moved from letter to letter, spelling out the name

'CAROLINE'.

"Thank you," said Seren. "Who was Caroline?"

The wind was getting up again, moaning impatiently as if trying to force its way into the attic. The pointer moved around erratically for a few moments, before spelling out the word 'LADY'. Seren gestured to Hannah to write it down.

"Okay, I'm not too sure what you mean by that, other than that she was female. Maybe you could tell us why she pushed you?"

Nothing happened for a few minutes, but the wind was now whining with even more intensity. The window pane rattled ominously and I heard what sounded like a tree branch scraping against an outside wall. Eventually the pointer began to move, this time spelling out the name 'JAMES'.

"Hmm, who was James?"

The word 'HUSBAND' was spelled out.

Seren frowned and rubbed her chin. "Alright, thank you," she said at last. "Now could you please tell us where you died?"

The candles flickered frenziedly as the wind appeared to have found its way in through some invisible opening and the attic door opened and slammed shut. We waited, drawn to the board. Then, very slowly, the pointer started to move. It spelled out the words 'HILLTOP HALL.'

Time seemed to stand still. Then I thought of something.

"Seren," I whispered, "Remember that time you felt something on the stairs!"

Seren looked at me and slowly nodded her head.

"I knew it!" she said with a satisfied grin.

CHAPTER 15

REVENGE

Wednesday afternoon found the four of us seated at a table in a secluded corner of the library. It had been Flo's idea to do some research on the history of Hilltop Hall. We managed (after some searching) to find some information which had been put together by some students as a history project many years previously. The file was dark green, very dusty, and looked like it hadn't been touched in a very long time. Someone with neat handwriting had written The History of Hilltop Hall on the cover. After a brief discussion, we decided it would be best to sneak the file out of the library and read it somewhere not so public. So Hannah shoved it in her bag and we went over to Attlee House where we had the privacy of my and Seren's room.

"Okay," said Seren as we settled down comfortably on the two beds, "why don't you read it out loud, Hannah? I think that would be the easiest way to do it."

"Sure," said Hannah agreeably. "Here goes:

'Hilltop Hall – an introduction

Once you have walked or driven up the winding hill, turn down the drive into the 150 acres of ancient parkland, and you will see appear amongst the trees one of England's glorious country houses, which is now a school. The small statue of a horse set in a neat box hedge garden welcomes visitors to the grand entrance of Hilltop Hall School. Hilltop Hall is an outstandingly beautiful red brick mansion in Jacobean, and eighteenth century styles. The gardens landscaped for the 1st Earl are gradually being restored by the Hilltop Hall Heritage Trust.

History

Hilltop Hall was built in the early 1620s as a hunting lodge. In 1637, following the latest fashions in architecture…'"

"Come on Hannah," moaned Seren, cutting her off, "I don't think we need to go that far back. Go to the section from about 1800 onwards."

"Okay," said Hannah. "Right, here it is:

'1846 - Lady Caroline Anson, Baroness Barton, marries James Fenn, MP, bringing to the marriage a large fortune and her title to Hilltop Hall.'"

"That must be her!" I said excitedly. "Lady Caroline Anson!"

Seren nodded, then said, "Carry on reading, Hannah."

"Okay, where was I? Oh yes, '1851 – James Fenn is created the first Earl of Kingsley.

1855 – A son is born, named Thomas Edward.

1857 – The compass gables were added by the great Captain Richard Gully.

1859 – The Dining Room was re-modelled in high Victorian fashion, classically proportioned to make a grand entertaining room.

1868 – The Kingsley family leave Hilltop Hall. There is much speculation as to why they left so suddenly. The house still belonged to them, but they moved to another, smaller residence.

1876 – Thomas Edward returns to Hilltop Hall.'"

"Wait a minute," said Flo, gesturing for Hannah to stop reading. "The family left the house in 1868, right? Miriam died in 1867. I wonder if there could have been some sort of connection between the two events."

We mulled this over for a few minutes, while the overhead light flickered mysteriously off and on a few times.

"It happened so long ago," I said. "But whatever happened was bad enough for Miriam's spirit to remain earthbound and restless all these years."

"Well she was murdered!" said Seren. "Pushed down a flight of stairs by this Caroline woman, who was probably never brought to justice!"

"But the big question," said Flo, "is: why did she do it?"

"Yes," said Seren. "And that's a question we need to put to Miriam."

***

That night the paranormal activity intensified. My bed shook and the bedroom light flickered on and off several times. Seren said it felt like someone was breathing down her neck. By morning we were exhausted and I wondered how Hannah and Flo had got on during the night.

I didn't have to wait long to find out; Seren and I bumped into them just before registration. We'd spotted them outside the cloakroom on the first floor. They were so absorbed in conversation that they didn't even notice us until I said, "Hi guys, what's up?"

"Oh!" said Flo, jumping nervously. "I didn't see you there!"

"Last night was pretty eventful," said Hannah, looking tense. "Flo and I were just swapping stories."

She went on to tell us that when she went to get a drink of water in the night, her feet had ended up in a large puddle of water as she stepped out of bed. She'd used a towel to mop it up, but as soon as she'd finished, another puddle appeared. It just kept happening until she eventually gave up and tried to go back to sleep. She also thought she heard whispering, even though her roommate, Lucy, was fast asleep.

But poor Flo seemed to have fared the worst. Sometime during the night, she'd woken to find herself floating a few feet above her bed! She was terrified and couldn't seem to get back down. She said she was certain she wasn't dreaming, although she did feel a bit strange, like her body was vibrating. Then, to make matters worse, Harriett woke up and screamed when she saw her. That's when Flo landed back on her bed with a thump.

"This morning I had to pretend I knew nothing about it!" she continued, wide-eyed. "When Harriett brought it up first thing, I told her she must have been dreaming!"

"That's called levitating," said Seren, looking serious.

"Whatever it is," said Flo with a shudder, "I do not want it to happen again. I was really freaked out!"

"Look guys," said Seren urgently, "things are obviously getting worse. We need to bring this whole thing to a close before..."

"Before what?" asked Hannah in alarm.

Seren bit her lip. "Um, just before anything really bad happens."

***

We decided to meet in the attic that night to try and put a stop to things once and for all. We were exhausted and taking strain, and I was sure our teachers must have noticed, because our schoolwork had begun to suffer. Miss Angelica gave me a concerned glance in Herbology, and I imagined she could somehow read my thoughts. On the one hand it was rather an unsettling feeling, but on the other I wished I could in some way let her know what was happening and ask for her advice.

The weather had turned cooler, and by Thursday evening it was drizzling steadily. We were in the attic by a quarter to twelve, sitting apprehensively on the old faded rug, with the Ouija board between us. Everything was quiet and the candles flickered steadily, but there was a definite sense of urgency as Seren did a quick protection ritual. I was feeling nervous and subconsciously fondled the little white pouch in my pocket.

Well we've certainly opened Pandora's Box, I thought to myself. *And now that the evil has escaped, the only thing left is hope.*

The rain was beginning to fall heavily on the roof as Seren prepared to start the séance, and my fingers trembled as I placed them on the wooden pointer.

"We are here tonight to speak with Miriam Marston," Seren began. "Miriam, if you are present, please give us a sign."

Nothing happened for a few minutes, but then the atmosphere began to change and the attic grew chilly. I felt the hairs on the back of my neck stand up, and a feeling of impending doom came over me. It was all quite overwhelming and for a moment I felt like getting up and running from the room. Then suddenly there was a terrifying gasp from Flo as she fell over backwards, clutching her throat! She writhed and thrashed about while making the most horrendous choking sounds. It looked like she was struggling against some unseen entity. Hannah became hysterical and began to cry, and I felt completely helpless and almost paralysed with fear. But thankfully Seren still had her wits about her and took charge of the situation.

"Miriam!" she screamed. "Stop that at once! You are only to use the board to communicate! Do you understand?"

Flo suddenly sat up, wide-eyed and white as a sheet. Everything was quiet except for the sound of the rain and Hannah's whimpering. Seren gave her a withering look before asking Flo if she was alright. Flo nodded and then, not wanting to waste any more time, Seren instructed us to put our fingers back on the pointer and keep them there. Poor Flo looked like she was in shock. Then after a few seconds, the pointer went zooming around the board before coming to rest on the word 'YES.'

"Thank you," said Seren. "Now, we need to know why Lady Caroline Anson pushed you down the stairs. Did it definitely have something to do with James?"

The pointer remained on the word 'YES."

"Okay," said Seren, "I'll take that as a yes. Now was there something going on between you and James?"

The pointer moved directly to the word 'NO.'

Seren sighed and looked thoughtful. Then she asked, "Did Lady Caroline think there was something going on between you and James."

The pointer almost flew to the word 'YES.'

"Thank you," said Seren, grinning. "Now we're getting somewhere."

She looked up at the rest of us and winked, looking very pleased with herself. Hannah, Flo and I just stared blankly back at her, still traumatised from what had just happened to Flo.

"Okay, so Lady Caroline was angry because she thought you and her husband were having an affair, so she pushed you down the stairs where you unfortunately met with your untimely death. Is this correct?"

An enormous and unexpected crack of thunder left us all shaking. The room turned icy cold and everything was silent except for Flo, who kept making a sound like she was clearing her throat. *Something had been trying to strangle her,* I thought in horror. Then Seren spoke again.

"Miriam," she said, "we'd really like to help you, but we need to know how? What exactly do you want?"

The pointer began to move, very slowly this time, as if making sure we took note of every single letter. The word spelled out was 'REVENGE'.

"I don't understand," said Seren, looking confused. "Both James and Caroline are dead. They died a very long time ago. There's nothing you can do now. You need to find peace by going towards the light."

An almighty crash sent us scrambling to our feet. The heavy wooden wardrobe had fallen over, and the large mirror on the front of it had smashed, leaving pieces of jagged glass strewn all over the floor. The atmosphere now felt extremely threatening, and my only thought was that it was time to leave. Then all of a sudden the candles went out. Panicked, Hannah stumbled towards the door, tugging frantically at the handle.

"It's stuck!" she screamed. "We're trapped!"

I started to feel sick. We were all very, very frightened. Seren fumbled around, looking for her lighter. Then after managing to relight the candles, she took a few deep breaths before telling us firmly to sit back down and put our fingers on the pointer. Having no other options, we reluctantly did as we were told.

Before Seren could even speak, the pointer started moving. For the first time it spelled out an entire sentence, which was: 'I WILL NOT LEAVE UNTIL I GET REVENGE.'

Shaking, we quickly moved the pointer to the word 'GOODBYE'

before Seren ran to try the door. Thankfully, it was no longer stuck and we were able to escape. At that moment, I never wanted to set foot back in that attic, ever.

CHAPTER 16

YOU ARE MINE TO KILL

On Friday afternoon none of us felt like doing anything. We strolled slowly down into town and sat around on some rocks by the stream. The rain had stopped and the sun was out, but the ground was still too soggy to sit on. We sat in silence, mulling over the previous night's frightening events. Things had been oddly quiet since we'd left the attic, but none of us could relax. Miriam's threats of revenge had us all on edge. My main thought was: *if she can't take revenge on Caroline, then who will be her victim?* The answer was obvious: it had to be one of us. Hannah and Flo both looked pale and worn out, and I was quite worried about them. At mealtimes, they just picked at their food and were beginning to look haggard and gaunt. I leaned down and swirled the water around aimlessly with a knobbly twig. *I really wish we'd never got involved with magic or the Ouija board or any of this stuff,* I thought to myself.

When we got back to school, Flo said she felt strongly that we should try to find pictures of the previous residents of Hilltop Hall. She said the thought just came to her suddenly, and she felt compelled to go to the library and see what she could find. Hannah was quite sullen and said she didn't feel like it.

"I just want to go and lie down," she said tiredly.

So Seren, Flo and I went to search the library for anything about Lady Caroline Anson or James Fenn, MP, or the first Earl of Kingsley. The first picture we found was of James Fenn, first Earl of Kingsley. His face bore a serious expression, he had short, light brown hair which was stuck down in a side parting, and a thick, curved moustache adorned his upper lip. He wore an old-fashioned suit and tie, with a white flower attached to one of the lapels.

"Eeuw!" said Seren. "He's not exactly what I'd call good looking! Why did they glue their hair down like that in those days?"

"Hmm," said Flo thoughtfully, "I think he looks quite dreamy. Like a real gentleman."

"Come on you guys!" I said impatiently. "Let's see if we can find a picture of this Caroline woman."

After a bit of searching, we eventually came across a book which looked promising. Flo scanned the index and smiled.

"Here we go," she said, "Lady Caroline Anson, page two hundred and twenty four."

Seren and I leaned in close as Flo flicked through the pages. Then we froze as our eyes came to rest on an old-fashioned portrait. Staring back at us was a fine, beautifully dressed young woman with pale skin, vivid green eyes and wavy auburn hair flowing out from under an elegant hat. I vaguely noticed that she was holding a teacup and saucer. But the only thought in my mind was that we were looking at a slightly older version of Flo.

"Oh my word!" gasped Seren, looking from the picture to Flo and back again.

Flo went white, dropped the book and swiftly fled. We quickly followed, catching up with her at the entrance to Churchill house. She turned and gave us a fleeting look before dashing up the stairs towards her room. Seren and I were quick, though, taking the steps two at a time so that we were just behind Flo when she opened her door, and she reluctantly let us in. Harriet was out, and the room looked normal 'til I noticed something out the corner of my eye. I nudged Seren, who followed my gaze. My first thought was: *we can't let Flo see this!* But it was too late. I caught Flo just as she sank to the floor in a faint. Then I looked back at the words on her dressing table mirror. In black eye liner was written: 'Florence Knowles, you are mine to kill.'

Seren and I gently picked up Flo and put her to bed. We cleaned the writing off the mirror and sat with her until she woke up. She looked very drowsy and said she just wanted to go back to sleep. Seren suggested that since Harriet was away for the weekend, I should stay with Flo. We both felt she shouldn't be left alone, so I agreed. Seren stayed with her for about half an hour while I went to fetch my overnight bag. When I returned, Flo seemed to be sleeping peacefully.

"It's Friday," Seren said as she left the room, "so I'll go fetch our phones. Then you can text me if anything happens."

Flo slept through supper, so I brought a couple of bread rolls and some fruit back to the room for her. She got shakily out of bed at around nine o'clock and went to take a shower. I lay on Harriet's bed, trying to escape into the idyllic fictional world of my book; it was all I could do to keep my fears at bay. I did my best to ignore the intermittent scratching noises that seemed to come from under Flo's bed, but when her radio suddenly crackled to life, I nearly jumped out of my skin!

I wonder how much more of this I can take, I wondered uncertainly.

After what felt like an eternity, Flo returned, wrapped in a white bath towel. Her eyes looked red and swollen, like she'd been crying.

"Lizzy," she said in a small, trembling voice, "I need to show you something."

Very slowly, she turned around and let the towel fall to the floor. I gasped and had to stifle a scream. All down her back were angry red scratch marks, as if someone had dragged their fingernails roughly over her skin.

"Oh Flo!" I cried, throwing my arms around her in a hug. "I'm so, so sorry. I never meant for any of this to happen. I just want it all to stop!"

I was in tears and felt so helpless. Shaking, I picked up my phone and was just about to text Seren, when I changed my mind. *No!* I thought angrily. *Seren hasn't helped at all! In fact, she's the one who got us into this mess in the first place!* But I knew I needed to turn to someone for help. So I made a decision.

"Flo!" I said urgently. "Get dressed! Just throw on any old thing, but be quick! We're going to pay someone a visit."

Flo looked puzzled but didn't argue as she walked passively over to her cupboard and took out some underwear and a navy blue jogging suit.

"Where are we going?" she asked meekly.

"I, um, I don't really want to say. It feels like the walls have ears. Just trust me Flo, okay?"

Flo nodded as she hurriedly dressed, flinching every time something touched her painful back. Then she sat down and pulled on a pair of trainers. I noticed how her fingers trembled as she did up the laces, while I hastily shrugged on a jumper and a pair of plimsolls. Then we left the building as quickly and quietly as we could.

***

The sky was still reasonably light, and we could easily see where we were going. The only drawback was that we risked being spotted, so I made sure I stayed behind the hedges and shrubs as much as possible, with Flo following close behind. It was a warm, windy night, and by the time we reached the woods I was feeling hot and sweaty. So, stopping in a clearing, I pulled off my jumper.

"It's so hot!" I exclaimed.

"Really?" asked Flo, frowning. "I'm freezing."

Just then there was a rustling in the branches above us, and a crow began to caw raucously. I felt my heartbeat quicken and started hurriedly along the path again, gesturing for Flo to follow. We hadn't gone further than a few paces, when I heard Flo cry out.

"Ouch!" she yelped. "I'm caught in something!"

I turned to see her trying to free herself from a large, unruly blackberry bush.

"Wait Flo!" I said as I jogged over. "Just keep still and I'll untangle you."

It took a good ten minutes and dozens of thorns in my fingers, but eventually Flo was free and we were on our way again. But we hadn't gone far before I had a strong and disturbing sensation that something was following us. I could feel its eyes boring into my back and the hairs on the back of my neck prickled. I grabbed Flo's arm and started to run. Then all of a sudden the trees came alive as the wind picked up strength. Branches swayed chaotically around us, as the whirling, swishing sound of wind through leaves filled the air. The noise soon grew deafening and the light was fading fast. Shifting shadows flitted from tree to tree, tormenting us. It's just little forest animals, I told myself valiantly. Just bunnies and squirrels and...

The wind suddenly dropped and a low menacing growl stopped us in our tracks. I felt paralysed with fear.

"What was that?" asked Flo, clutching my arm in terror.

"I, d,don't know," I said, almost hyperventilating.

Just then we heard another growl, this time louder and filled with foreboding.

"Run!" screamed Flo, and, holding hands, we fled down the path as fast as we could, not stopping till we reached our destination. We stood panting for a while, leaning against a wall while trying to get our breaths back.

When our heartbeats had returned to a rate slightly resembling normal, we heard a meow as Miss Angelica's cat sauntered over and rubbed her soft furry body against our legs. It felt strangely comforting, and I bent down to stroke her. Then unexpectedly the front door opened and we heard Miss Angelica's voice.

"Shadow!" she called, "Come pretty girl! Shadow!"

Flo and I looked at each other; she was obviously calling the cat. It was time to make our move.

"Miss Angelica!" I called out.

"Who's there?" she asked, sounding startled.

"It's me, Eliza! And Flo's also here," I said as we approached.

"Girls!" she exclaimed, "What brings you here in the middle of the night? Did you come through the woods in the dark?"

"Miss Angelica," I said urgently. "Please, we really need to talk to you."

"Of course. Do come inside."

CHAPTER 17
NO TIME TO LOSE

The cottage was gloomy inside, the only light coming from a small cluster of candles. Miss Angelica told us to make ourselves comfortable, so we sank, exhausted, into the two chairs, and proceeded to tell her everything. The further we got in our story, the more concerned Miss Angelica looked. By the time we had related the events of earlier that evening, she was pacing the floor of her little sitting room, wringing her hands and shaking her head. It was both strange and unsettling to see Miss Angelica like that - she was usually so calm and serene.

She listened intently without interrupting, but now she turned to face us. I could see the worry and anxiety in her eyes, and it frightened me.

"Oh girls!" she said at last. "I don't know quite how to say this, but you've got yourselves into an exceedingly dangerous situation. I am a Wiccan. My type of witchcraft is a spiritual, nature-loving practice that teaches peace and responsibility. The spells that wiccans perform are of healing, love, harmony, wisdom, creativity, peace and understanding. I've always kept my distance from the dark side. Sure, I know about it. But I'm not familiar with the procedures you need to follow in order to rid yourselves of whatever negative entity has somehow attached itself to you."

Flo and I sat quietly and listened, relieved to be in the presence of someone who had some understanding of what we were going through. Miss Angelica was silent for a few minutes, stroking her chin and sighing deeply. Eventually she looked up and scurried over to a little wooden cabinet. Opening a drawer, she took out a small fabric-covered book and began to flip through it.

"Ah!" she said at last, "Here it is. I know a man - a shaman - who lives just outside town. He's supposed to be quite knowledgeable about the practice of uh, evicting, you could say, unwanted entities. Let me give him a ring and see what he can do."

Flo and I listened as Miss Angelica disclosed the main points of our problem to the man on the telephone. Eventually she finished with the words: "Yes I agree - the sooner the better. Alright, I'll let them know. Thank you."

She put the phone down and turned to face us.

"Right girls," she said, clasping her hands nervously in front of her chest, "Shinpi says there's no time to lose. He'll be here in about twenty minutes. In the meantime, you need to find your two friends and go up to the attic. Shinpi and I will meet you there."

The thought of walking back through the woods caused a tight knot to form in my stomach, and Flo didn't look happy either. Miss Angelica must have sensed our trepidation, because she told us to hang on a second while she went and got something. She returned a minute later with a shiny gold pouch.

"Take this," she said solemnly. "It will keep you safe."

Then, ushering us out the door, she said she'd walk as far as the entrance to the woods with us. The night was now still and completely dark. I felt safe with Miss Angelica, and wished she could accompany us all the way back to school. But all too soon we were standing before the woods, the profound blackness therein appearing to conceal all manner of malevolent creatures. We paused for a moment while our eyes grew accustomed to the darkness. Then Miss Angelica, who I noticed had been carrying a wand, now took it and drew the shape of a pentagram in the air between Flo and me. While doing it, she said the words:

"Hail fair moon,
Ruler of the night;
Guard these girls
Until the light."

Then, arm in arm, Flo and I set off, comforted by the protection spell, but still very nervous of what might lie before us.

***

We arrived back at school breathless but safe and sound. Our journey through the woods had been one mad, frantic dash, punctuated by frequent shouts of "Look out!" as we came across hazardous tree roots in our path. We had run, hand in hand, with Flo holding on tight to the gold protection pouch, not looking anywhere but straight in front of us. Now, hidden behind a well-manicured hedge in the school grounds, we paused to discuss our next steps. It was decided that I should go and call Seren, and Flo would call Hannah, and we'd all meet up in the attic as quickly as we could.

Seren was surprised to see me, and wanted to know what had happened. I gave her a much abbreviated version of the night's events so far, and at first she was really angry.

"I told you to text me if anything happened!" she hissed. "But you just went off without saying anything and now we've got all these people interfering! And what about our pact?"

"Look Seren," I said, feeling my anger rise, "this isn't a game anymore! We are all in real danger! Right now I don't care what you think. And I don't care about that stupid pact. I just want this whole nightmare to end!"

Shaking, I turned to leave.

"Wait!" called Seren as I reached the door, "I'll go with you."

When we got to the attic, Hannah and Flo were already waiting. But they were too afraid to actually go into the attic, so they sat on the wooden steps, looking weary. They seemed relieved to see us. Seren and I also sat down on the steps, and there the four of us waited in nervous anticipation until Miss Angelica and Shinpi arrived about fifteen minutes later.

Shinpi was a short man with a pointy little beard who wore his long grey hair tied back in a ponytail. He had on a black shirt, black jeans, and black shoes. I had imagined he'd be dressed in robes or animal skins and beads - witch doctor stuff - but he looked quite normal. He greeted us and explained that he was there to do a cleansing ritual, which would hopefully rid us of any unwanted or negative entities that might be hanging around. He spoke in a gentle, reassuring voice, but I could sense the tension in his body.

When we entered the attic, everyone's attention was drawn to the old wardrobe, which still lay face down on the floor amid shards of glass. Miss Angelica and Shinpi exchanged troubled glances. Then Shinpi lit some white candles and told us to form a circle in the middle of the room, while he took numerous items out of his duffel bag and placed them on the fold-out table. He then went over to the little window, climbed onto the chair which still stood below it, and opened it as wide as it would go. Then he issued each of us with a clear quartz crystal, which he said would help absorb any negative energy. We slowly began to relax, as Shinpi appeared confident and knowledgeable, and did everything in a calm manner.

He began the ritual by saying a kind of prayer asking for protection, before lighting what he called a smudge stick, which was a bunch of dried sage tied tightly together. He waved the smoke from the burning herbs around his whole body, back and front, from head to foot. Then he did the same to each of us in turn. After that he gestured for us to follow him around the room, where he waved the smouldering smudge stick around in the air, swirling it into every nook and cranny until the whole attic was filled with the sweet smell of burning sage. We then followed him out the door and down the wooden stairs. I wondered where he was going. Down the narrow staircases we went, until Shinpi stopped on the landing where Seren had first sensed the troubled spirit of Miriam. He waved the smoke around the landing three times before making his way back up to the attic, with the five of us following close behind.

Back in the attic, Shinpi put the smudge stick into a small bowl and snuffed it out. Then he told us to form a circle around him on the carpet while he meditated for a few minutes. So we sat and joined hands, our eyes on Shinpi as he sat in silence with his eyes closed. After a while his body began to twitch disturbingly, and the atmosphere underwent a change. The air became cold and a swift breeze blew in through the open window.

Shinpi suddenly opened his eyes, which were now filled with anxiety.

"I'm afraid there's still something here," he said quietly. "I sense a very stubborn entity - even a bit hostile - and this unfortunately calls for more, err, let's say aggressive steps."

It was now so cold that I could see the condensation of my breath. Then all of a sudden Flo let go of my hand and screamed in agony.

"My arm!" she wailed. "It felt like teeth sinking in!"

Shinpi and Miss Angelica immediately held up a candle to look at Flo's arm, while we all craned our necks to see what had happened. In the dim light I was horrified to see a large bite mark on the soft white skin of Flo's inner arm. The flesh around the bite seemed to swell painfully as I watched. Miss Angelica put her arm around Flo's shoulders as Shinpi got up and went over to the table where he'd unpacked various items. He busied himself for a few minutes while the rest of us comforted Flo as best we could. Then Shinpi asked us to join him at the table.

A very old, worn book with a scruffy black cover lay on the table, opened to a faded page which was filled with elaborate handwriting. Beside it were two wooden bowls, one filled with soil and the other with water. There was also a black candle, a sharp, narrow blade, a pen and four small pieces of paper.

"Alright everyone," Shinpi said at last, "I've set up the items needed for a banishing ritual. I was hoping it wouldn't come to this, but..." His voice trailed off as he cast his eyes down and took a deep breath. Then he said, "Can someone please tell me the name of the spirit or entity you think you made contact with in this room."

"Um, it's a girl in spirit called Miriam Marston," said Seren.

Shinpi nodded, thanked her, and wrote down the name on each of the four pieces of paper. It was now so cold that we were all shivering. I watched as Shinpi turned each piece of paper over and drew a pentagram on the other side. Then he carefully carved Miriam's name into the candle using the sharp blade. The atmosphere was distinctly unpleasant, and I couldn't wait for the whole thing to be over. But I had a sinking feeling that Miriam – if in fact the entity really was her - might put up one last fight. I hoped I was wrong.

Shinpi mumbled off what sounded like some sort of verse, before lighting the black candle and holding one of the pieces of paper in the flame. While the paper burned, Shinpi said in a loud and commanding voice, "I banish Miriam Marston with the power of Fire. So mote it be!"

Suddenly the sound of woeful wailing filled the room. It seemed to come from everywhere, echoing off the walls and causing a distinct vibration in the air around us. Working quickly, Shinpi picked up another piece of paper and buried it in the bowl of soil.

"I banish Miriam Marston with the power of Earth. So mote it be!" he bellowed over the noise.

We waited uneasily, anticipating a response. A moment later the wailing ceased and the candle began to billow thick black smoke, causing Flo to start choking. She coughed and spluttered as Miss Angelica guided her away from the smoke and over to the open window. Shinpi, picking up the third piece of paper, hurriedly continued with the ritual. He seemed to be losing his sense of calm, and that scared me.

As he placed the paper in the bowl of water, he said, "I banish Miriam Marston with the power of Water. So mote it be!"

The paper floated on the water and the candle stopped billowing black smoke. The temperature in the room began to rise and Miss Angelica and Flo returned to the table. I allowed myself to feel a slight glimmer of hope. Then Shinpi picked up the last piece of paper and went over to the window. He climbed onto the chair and stretched his arm out into the still night air.

"I banish M…" Shinpi began, but before he could say any more, the chair started hopping from side to side. Looking panicked, he clung onto the window frame to keep his balance. Then suddenly a violent gust of wind blew in, threatening to blow out the candles. This mysterious wind quickly grew in strength, becoming more and more powerful, until we had to grab hold of the items on table to keep them from being blown around. The roar of the wind was now deafening and was beginning to take on a sinister moan. Holding onto the ancient-looking book, my hair billowing out in all directions, I glanced over at Flo, who appeared to be resisting something that was trying to pull her away. Her hands were wrapped tightly around one of the table legs, and her body was stretched out straight, with both feet in the air!

"Flo!" I screamed, dropping the book, "Grab hold of my hand!"

As she did so, I heard Shinpi's voice over the howl of the wind.

"I banish Miriam Marston with the power of Wind! So mote it be!" he roared determinedly.

There was a long, drawn-out, ear-piercing shriek which gradually faded and grew distant. It echoed like someone screaming while falling down an empty well. We listened in shocked silence until all of a sudden the wind dropped and everything went quiet. Flo collapsed on the floor in an exhausted heap as the rest of us watched the black candle finally burn down and go out.

CHAPTER 18

LESSONS LEARNED

We all sat around the old pine kitchen table which we'd helped Miss Angelica carry out into her garden. A pretty floral cloth covered the scrubbed wooden surface, on which lay pretty mismatched china plates laden with cakes and sandwiches. Bees buzzed, birds chirped, and the sweet scent of honeysuckle filled the air. The summer sun shone out of a clear blue sky and we chatted happily, feeling the excitement of the long summer holiday ahead.

All the paranormal activity had ceased after that last night in the attic, and we had gradually gone back to living our lives much as we had done before becoming involved in the supernatural. The only difference was that the four of us were now closer than ever after all we'd been through together. Seren reluctantly admitted that Dylan had led her down a path she would have been better off avoiding, and the two of them eventually broke up. Flo still suffered from nightmares, but was coping much better since seeing a counsellor. All in all, we seemed to have come through our ordeal quite satisfactorily, and with a newfound appreciation for the more mundane things in life. I think we'd had enough excitement to last us a very long time!

"Why do you think we attracted a negative spirit?" I asked Miss Angelica, as we sat around enjoying the picnic. "Do you think that by doing those revenge spells we somehow caused the bad luck to come back to us?"

Miss Angelica looked thoughtful as she chewed her food.

"It's hard to say," she said at last. "From what you've told me, I'm not even sure those spells you girls did worked. I mean, when you think about it, the results could just be put down to coincidence. But when you start messing around with Ouija boards and doing séances and things like that, you're actually opening a door to the spirit world. Think about it like an internet chat room if it helps. There's nothing wrong with talking to people 'til one of them turns out to be a murderer or a paedophile. You don't know who is what when you enter that room. And the same is true of the Ouija board. It's also a form of voluntary possession. In order to get the spirit to contact you through the board by moving the pointer, you basically have to give up your will - it's the only way for them to work through you. The spirit isn't moving the pointer, but it's causing you to move it with your hands by way of possession. Once you've opened up the Ouija board, there's no telling what's going to try to make contact. You don't know who or what is communicating with you, or what its purpose is."

"So we might not have even been communicating with the spirit of Miriam Marston?" I asked incredulously.

Miss Angelica frowned. "Look, I won't pretend to have all the answers. But I know that contact is often made with beings residing in the very lowest levels of the astral planes. The lower in the Astral worlds the being, the lower is their Energy vibration, usually indicating a correspondingly low level of trust. They'll frequently claim to be Angels, Archangels, famous people or even God, while others will claim to be deceased people known to the Ouija board sitters. I'm not saying the spirit of Miriam Marston didn't try to make contact – maybe she did. But I wouldn't be surprised if a dark, negative entity which was lurking around, looking for an opportunity, decided to impersonate her. Then, as it fed off the energy of you four girls and became stronger, it was able to work towards its ultimate goal: possession. Remember the 'Shadows?'"

"Wow," I said, shaking my head, "That's some scary stuff. I really wish we'd listened when you tried to warn us about negative entities and all that. We just got so sucked in to the whole thing. It seemed to have a kind of hold on us." I shuddered at the memory.

"Sometimes," Miss Angelica said kindly, "people only learn from experience."

"I suppose you're right," I said, feeling a bit ashamed. "But I really regret it now."

"You girls are lucky though," she added seriously. "Never forget that. You learned your lesson, but things could have ended very differently."

I looked over at Flo, who was stroking Shadow and telling her what a pretty little kitty she was. I was pleased to see her looking so relaxed and at ease again. I didn't even want to think about what might have happened to her. Or to any of us for that matter.

The Toffees were still the same. They continued to make rude or sarcastic comments from time to time, but we'd found more constructive ways to deal with them.

I gazed up at the clear blue sky as a crow cawed overhead. We'd learned some important life lessons, that's for sure. And one of them can be summed up in the words of Douglas Horton:

'While seeking revenge, dig two graves — one for yourself.'

ABOUT THE AUTHOR

Mila Lightfoot had an extraordinarily adventurous childhood growing up in the South African countryside. She now lives with her husband and three children in the beautiful Yorkshire Dales where they have a menagerie of animals, big and small. As a qualified Master Herbalist, Mila is interested in plant cures and believes in a Holistic way of life.

This is Mila's third book. She has written and illustrated two books for children, and this is her first novel for teenagers. Her other books are *The Very Greedy Boy* and *The Wicked Tale of Alfie Jones*.

7387226R00097

Printed in Great Britain
by Amazon.co.uk, Ltd.,
Marston Gate.